*A
Harlequin
Romance*

OTHER
Harlequin Romances
by LUCY GILLEN

Many of these titles are available at your local bookseller,
or through the Harlequin Reader Service.

For a free catalogue listing all available Harlequin Romances,
send your name and address to:

HARLEQUIN READER SERVICE,
M.P.O. Box 707, Niagara Falls, N.Y. 14302
Canadian address: Stratford, Ontario, Canada.

or use order coupon at back of book.

SUMMER SEASON

by

LUCY GILLEN

HARLEQUIN BOOKS   TORONTO
WINNIPEG

Original hard cover edition published in 1971
by Mills & Boon Limited

© Lucy Gillen 1971

SBN 373-01711-1

Harlequin edition published August, 1973

Printed in Canada

CHAPTER ONE

EARLY summer, Sheena thought, was quite the nicest time of the year, before the visitors who came flocking into Sandlea inevitably overflowed into Lea Bay. True, it was only an adventurous few who found their way along the tree-lined road to the reserved tranquillity of Lea Bay, but the residents of that select little community preferred to keep their rather opulent isolation intact and even half a dozen interlopers were too many.

The bay itself sparkled richly in the June sun, and the green of the trees and flowering shrubs that shielded each house from its neighbour and from the quiet road was as yet fresh and delicate without the dusty, tired look that the season would bring. Even this far from the seaside town the months at the height of summer were known as the season, although referred to with less enthusiasm than by the hoteliers in Sandlea.

There was sufficient space between the shrubs in the garden to give a good view and Sheena was so engrossed with the picture it made, framed in the high wide window, that she failed to hear the door open behind her and started almost guiltily, giving a little squeak of surprise when the newcomer spoke.

'Didn't you hear me coming?'

Sheena smiled at him and shook her head. John Cameron had been her guardian for almost as long as she could remember and there was a rapport between them that many a father and child would have envied. He was her mother's brother and he and his young wife had fostered Sheena ever since her parents parted and later died, then, tragically, his own wife had died and Sheena had been his only close family for nearly twenty years.

He came across to join her by the window, his dark, good-looking face incredibly like his niece's as he laid his cheek briefly against hers in greeting. 'I nearly jumped out of my skin,' Sheena admitted laughingly. 'I was admiring the view and got carried away, I'm afraid.'

'That view!' He smiled at her teasingly. 'After nearly fifteen years you should be used to it by now, but there, I suppose your artistic eye never grows tired, does it?'

'Not very often,' Sheena allowed. 'It's constantly changing and never the same twice together. Look at it now, for instance, with the light greens of the trees and shrubs and the – the gold colour of the sea in the sun, it's enough to inspire anyone.'

'But you're not inspired enough to put brush to canvas,' he teased her, laughing at her grimace of reproach. 'I know,' he added apologetically, 'you're having a temporary off time at the moment – sorry, I forgot.' He dropped a kiss, lightly, on her forehead and turned back into the room. 'I hope Mrs. Goodenough isn't too long with our dinner, I'm famished!'

Sheena reluctantly left the glitter of the sea for the shadowed coolness of the room, her eyes momentarily blinded by the contrast. 'It smelled delicious when I came past the kitchen just now,' she said. 'I think we've only been waiting for you to come before we start.'

'I tried to persuade Suna to join us,' her uncle told her as they went into the sunny dining-room across the hall, 'but she has other fish to fry, it seems.'

'A dinner date, maybe?' Sheena suggested, mildly malicious, her eyes dancing mischief, for she knew the unlikelihood of any such thing.

John Cameron had known Suna Blane for almost five years now and their original friendship had gradually developed into something more serious. Sheena had great

6

hopes of the outcome, although so far he had not proposed. She felt sure enough of that because she felt so certain that had he done so he would have been accepted without hesitation.

Suna was a stunningly attractive widow of thirty-six, a successful commercial artist and obviously very fond of John Cameron, so the match would be suitable in every way, Sheena thought, if only her uncle would ask her to marry him. It would mean that he would perhaps give more time to his home life and less to the business that occupied him so much of the time.

The dark eyes, so incredibly like her own, smiled down at Sheena as he sat down at the table and she knew he was probably quite aware of her train of thought. 'It wasn't a dinner date,' he informed her, with as much certainty as she felt herself, 'it's a meeting of the Ladies' Committee. Suna's becoming increasingly immersed in good works lately for some reason or other.'

'Maybe because you neglect her so shamefully,' Sheena retorted, and her uncle laughed.

'Neglect can only be applied to something belonging,' he told her, 'and Suna is a free agent.'

She had never tried such open tactics before and she thought it surprised him, although he showed more signs of being amused by it than annoyed.

'Not from choice,' she told him, deciding to strike again while the opportunity was there.

He glanced at her warily as she picked up her serviette. 'You seem to be well informed,' he remarked. 'Better than I am, apparently.'

Sheena smiled, detecting no resentment in the words. 'Maybe I am,' she agreed. 'I like Suna and I think I know her fairly well by now, also it's the kind of thing a woman notices and a man doesn't.'

'I see.' He smiled, but she thought he took the state-

7

ment quite seriously.

Mrs. Goodenough's arrival with their dinner halted the exchange at that point, but Sheena thought her own uncharacteristic insistence had given him food for thought and that, at least, was something. She smiled inwardly at the idea that perhaps if she persevered she could make him see sense before Suna gave up in despair.

'The Madocs are expecting a visitor for the season,' John announced, when they were alone again, and Sheena looked up in surprise.

'Surely not,' she said. 'No one in Lea Bay takes visitors, and especially Uncle George.'

Her uncle smiled, pleased to have shocked her, however briefly. 'It's a relative, so Gwyn said,' he told her. 'He's appearing at the Majestic in Sandlea and he's staying with George and Gwyn rather than at a hotel.'

'Appearing?' Sheena frowned over the word. 'You mean he's actually in the summer show?' Her uncle nodded. 'Well, who is he, anyone well-known? They have some big names at the Majestic, though I'd no idea the Madocs were well connected in *that* direction.'

John Cameron laughed, enjoying his moment of suspense. 'His name's Van Goalan, according to Gwyn,' he told her, and watched her blank stare of disbelief with twinkling eyes.

'Van Goalan!' Sheena could scarcely believe her ears. 'Do you mean to say he's actually related to Gwyn and I never knew?'

'Evidently,' her uncle agreed, enjoying her surprise.

'But it's unbelievable!' She eyed him for a moment suspiciously. 'Are you sure you didn't misunderstand him, Uncle John?'

John Cameron shook his head. 'No, I didn't,' he insisted. 'And I'm surprised you didn't know, considering all the time you spend with Gwyn.'

'Not all that much time,' Sheena denied, 'but of all the – he might have told me he was related to someone like Van Goalan. He knows I – I'm an admirer of his.'

'A fan, Gwyn said,' John Cameron smiled.

'An admirer,' Sheena insisted. 'It's typical of him, of course,' she added resignedly, 'he wouldn't think anything like that was of any importance.'

Her uncle looked across the table at her quizzically, obviously finding her attitude amusing. 'I must admit he was rather off-hand about it,' he admitted, 'so I gathered he wasn't very impressed himself, but he seemed to think you would be.'

'Then he's not disappointed,' Sheena declared shortly, visualizing Gwyn Madoc's rather condescending amusement at the idea.

She had known Gwyn, and his father George, ever since they had moved to Lea Bay over twelve years before, taking the huge, white-painted house just next but one to her uncle's. The two older men had become friends quite quickly, partly due to some quite heavy investments George Madoc had made in her uncle's export and shipping company, and when Gwyn had declined the university place open to him, John Cameron had willingly taken him into the firm. It was a decision he had never had cause to regret, for Gwyn had worked hard, going through every phase of the business until, at thirty, he was now a junior partner in the firm.

If Sheena ever gave it a thought at all she would have been the first to admit that she took Gwyn rather for granted. Someone who was always there and would always be there, in fact she found it difficult to remember when he had *not* been there. They argued incessantly, mostly because he refused to take her career as an artist seriously, although she had received a gratifying amount of success in quite a short time. They went swimming and sailing together and sometimes dancing and to dinner, but mostly he treated her with the amused tolerance of an elder brother.

The fact that he was related to anyone as exciting and well-known as Van Goalan had come as a complete surprise to her and she raised the subject again as they ate their dinner. 'I think Gwyn might have told me about Van Goalan,' she said. 'He must have known for some time that he was coming, yet he never said a word about it.'

'Especially when he knows you're a fan of his,' John Cameron suggested with a wry smile, and she frowned her dislike of the noun.

'I think he's very good,' she told him, managing to convey her disapproval, 'and very versatile. He's equally good as an actor and a singer. He's also very attractive,' she added, half defiant, 'which is probably why Gwyn is so scathing about him.'

'Oh, I wouldn't say scathing exactly,' her uncle denied, still smiling to himself, 'he was just – well, off-hand, but if the man's a relative you'd hardly expect him to be all that impressed, would you? The novelty of having a celebrity in the family will have worn off by now, I expect.'

'How much of a relative is he?' Sheena asked.

Her uncle shrugged, as off-hand as he declared Gwyn Madoc to be. 'I think he said he was a second cousin or something somewhere on his mother's side.'

Sheena had never known Mrs. Madoc, she was already dead when Gwyn and his father moved to Lea Bay, but she had seen a painting of her which hung in the sitting-room and she had to admit to a certain detectable likeness in the painted features of the woman in the portrait and the good looks of Van Goalan.

She was even forced to recognize some similarity to Gwyn, although he could never be called good-looking, his features were much too rugged and stubbornly self-confident, but he had the colouring common to all three, fair hair and blue eyes. Even there, though, Gwyn had some difference, for his mother and Van Goalan had silky-looking straight hair that lay smoothly, while his was coarse and, where it grew above his ears and in the nape of his neck, very slightly curly.

'Did you say he's staying for the whole season?' Sheena asked, and her uncle smiled at her obvious interest.

'I did,' he agreed, and arched a meaningful brow at her. 'Gwyn thought you'd be pleased about *that*, he also wondered if you'd like to go to lunch the Sunday after next.'

'Oh?' Sheena looked at him suspiciously. Although invitations to lunch at the Madoc house were not infrequent, they more usually came from George Madoc than his son.

'To meet the famous heart-throb,' her uncle teased, and Sheena lifted her chin defensively.

'Treating me like a gooey-eyed schoolgirl, as usual,' she said. 'He would!'

'I rather think he was trying to please you for once,' John Cameron told her, mildly reproachful, 'but you don't have to go if you'd rather not. I said I'd ask you first before I accepted for you in case you'd made some other arrangements.'

'Knowing full well I hadn't,' Sheena said with a smile of understanding, 'but thanks for thinking of it all the same, Uncle John.' She looked at him questioningly. 'Are you going, or aren't you invited?'

'Oh yes, rather, and Suna too. I know she shares your admiration of Van Goalan, but I wouldn't commit any of us until I'd seen you first.'

'And I can't very well refuse without appearing horribly selfish and ungracious.'

'Do you want to refuse?'

She shook her head, smiling wryly. 'You and Gwyn know quite well I won't refuse,' she said, acknowledging the fact inevitably. 'Of course I'll go, Uncle John, I'd love to. I've never seen a real live celebrity close at hand before.'

Sheena dressed with extra care for lunch at the Madoc house that Sunday. Always meticulous with her dress when the occasion demanded it, she spent even longer than usual and yet was still ready in good time so that she had time to consider the result.

She gazed at her reflection for some time in the mirror, critical but not too much so. There was no conceit in the gaze, although it would have been forgivable if there had been. The eyes that surveyed her image were deep, dark brown and thick-fringed with dark lashes set in a face almost childishly lovely at times. Living so close to the sea always as she did, her skin had a soft golden colour that, combined with the long, almost black hair, gave her a rather exotic look that was enchanting.

The dress she had chosen to wear, a deep golden yellow and simply cut, added to the effect and altogether, she thought, she was quite pleased with her appearance, especially with the high-piled hair-style she had managed to achieve after much effort. A wry smile as she turned away from the mirror recognized the fact that the famous visitor she had taken so much trouble for would probably not even notice her.

Presumably Mrs. Groome, the Madocs' cook-house-keeper, was busy with lunch, for Gwyn himself admitted them when they arrived and he at least registered her unusually sophisticated image with a brow that expressed volumes.

He sought her eyes unerringly, his own gleaming wickedly as he winked at her. 'All dressed up for the big occasion,' he teased. 'Prepare to swoon, for your big moment is at hand!'

He laughed at her discouraging frown. 'I'm *not* an impressionable teenager,' she told him shortly, as he took her coat, 'so stop trying to impress me, Gwyn.'

Her uncle, glancing back as he walked on with Suna, knew how she was being teased, but he merely smiled tolerantly as always, while Suna Blane arched understanding brows but also said nothing.

'Oh, come on, Tuppence, be impressed,' Gwyn urged, and she bit her lip at the familiar nickname from her childhood. It had been her huge dark brown eyes that had inspired him to call her that and, at first, she had not objected; only now when she was older did she feel that she should be afforded the deference of her proper name. Gwyn, of course, did not see her reason or would not admit it.

'Don't call me that,' she told him, 'especially in front of a – a stranger.'

'You think he might laugh at you?' he guessed, his brown face crinkled into a laugh that both teased and consoled her. 'Don't worry, Tuppence, I won't do anything to spoil your big moment.' For a second his glance flicked over her face and the high-piled hair, then he shook his head. 'You don't have to worry about first impressions,' he told her, 'you look like a million dollars. Come on, gorgeous.'

Her uncle and his companion were already sipping drinks and talking animatedly to a tall, fair-haired man the other side of the room when she went in with Gwyn, and George Madoc came over from the group, smiling affectionately at her as he always did. He doted on Sheena and made almost as much of her as her uncle did.

13

He was a remarkably good-looking man even at well over fifty, darker by far than his son, though he too had blue eyes that swept over her admiringly, much as Gwyn's had done. 'Sheena my dear, how lovely you look.' He kissed her before handing her a drink. 'It's that dress that helps, of course, you have such perfect taste.'

Sheena smiled, her eyes straying involuntarily to the stranger talking to her uncle and Suna. 'Thank you, Uncle George.'

Gwyn grinned knowingly, following her gaze, and winking at his father. 'It's not us she's all dressed up for, Pop, it's our celebrated kinsman, isn't it, Tuppence?'

Afraid that the man referred to would overhear, Sheena flicked him a look of reproach which he greeted with his usual grin.

'Well, of course it is,' George Madoc agreed with an understanding smile. 'Come over and meet Van, Sheena dear, he's been hearing all about you.'

It was Gwyn's arm that encircled her shoulders as they moved over to join the group by the window, and his smile anticipated her nervousness. 'Don't worry, he won't eat you,' he whispered in her ear, and laughed softly at her indignant frown. His arm drew her into the group and his smile might almost have been proprietorial as he introduced her. 'Here she is,' he told his cousin, 'the dishiest gal in Lea Bay – Sheena Hastings. Sheena – Van Goalan.'

'Miss Hastings, I'm delighted to meet you at last.' The handclasp was firm and strong and only as long as politeness demanded, but in the few seconds of its existence Sheena felt a rapid increase in her pulse rate and a rather dizzying sensation in her brain.

It was her first encounter with anyone from show business, especially anyone as well known as Van Goalan, and she would have thought herself far too sensible to be affected by the mere fact of shaking hands, but there was an indefinable something about this man that explained his fabulous success in his profession.

She had seen him many times in various mediums and yet had always counted him as someone not quite real, as such people often appear from a distance, yet here he was, real enough to make her feel slightly lightheaded at meeting him.

Looking at him more objectively, she supposed he was rather shorter than she had expected, but that could have been the proximity of Gwyn's six feet two inches which dwarfed quite a lot of people, but the almost perfectly proportioned features and the handsome head with its blond hair were exactly as she had seen them so many times. Only his complexion seemed disappointingly pale, but no doubt a season by the sea would soon alter that.

'I – I'm delighted to meet you.' She was aware of Gwyn's arm tightening on her shoulders and looked up briefly at the bright mockery of his gaze before returning her attention to Van Goalan.

'Sheena is a fan of yours from way back, Van,' Gwyn told his cousin, and Sheena felt the instinctive urge to curl up and hide when the good-looking face smiled understanding. It was as if he saw her as just another adoring schoolgirl, one of thousands, and for a moment she hated Gwyn for making her appear so.

'I dislike being called a fan,' she declared, shrugging the encircling arm from her shoulders, 'but I *am* an admirer of yours, Mr. Goalan.'

'Then I'm flattered,' he told her, the blue eyes adding sincerity to the words. 'Perhaps now we've met we can enjoy mutual pleasure, Miss Hastings. Gwyn has been telling me how lovely you are and frankly, until now, I doubted his honesty. Seeing you I must allow I owe him an apology. He was very truthful.'

The compliment was unexpected and so charmingly paid, but it was so unlike Gwyn to have been so flattering that Sheena glanced up at him curiously and surprised an uncharacteristic look of sheepishness about him which he endeavoured to disguise with a grin that was more than half defiance.

'Gwyn exaggerates,' she declared.

'No, indeed he doesn't.' The slight half bow, she felt, was delightfully gallant and matched exactly the almost imperceptible accent which, until now, she had to confess she had not noticed. It was another point that added to his already considerable attraction.

'You're not English, are you, Mr. Goalan?' Suna Blane voiced Sheena's own curiosity, and Van Goalan smiled slowly, shaking his head.

'Only half, I'm afraid, Mrs. Blane,' he said, as if it was cause for regret. 'My father is Dutch and I was born in Holland, though I had thought it undetectable by now. I felt sure my accent was completely gone, but obviously I was wrong.'

'Really?' Suna looked interested. 'I'd no idea, although I suppose your name should have told me something, shouldn't it? And really your accent *is* almost disappeared. Your English is more perfect than that of some English people I know.'

'Possibly,' Van Goalan agreed with a wry smile, 'wasn't it Shaw who mentioned that point in Pygmalion? It can sometimes be as much a betrayal of origin as an accent, I think.'

'I don't imagine the ladies are complaining,' Gwyn assured him with a grin. 'They'd still find you irresistible even if you used your own name, Van. It's the glamour they go for.'

'No doubt,' his cousin agreed goodnaturedly, 'but I think I stand more chance than I would have done as

Pieter Van Goalan.' It was obvious, Sheena thought, that the two men were on excellent terms and she wondered how two such different characters could be compatible.

'But he draws the line at being called Pete,' Gwyn added facetiously, and Suna nodded.

'Strictly speaking,' she said, 'I suppose I should have called you Mr. Van Goalan, not Mr. Goalan?'

A smile dismissed either as necessary. 'I'd much prefer it if you called me Van,' he said. 'I'm used to it as a christian name now and I'd much rather you used it.' The words may have been addressed to Suna, but the blue eyes were fixed on Sheena and she felt the warm tinge of colour in her cheeks. Van Goalan, she told herself, was even more devastatingly attractive at close quarters than his recorded image implied, and she would need to have all her wits about her to keep a level head.

'You've made a big hit with the visiting pasha,' Gwyn informed her the following evening when he saw her on the beach and sat down beside her uninvited.

Sheena had been quite happy sitting there alone, hugging her knees and watching the tide roll in, lace-edged and lazy in the evening sun. She had been as discouraging as she could when Gwyn arrived, but guessed she had wasted her time. Gwyn did not take easily to hints or to discouragement, in fact he was rather more inclined to thrive on the latter.

It was getting on for nine o'clock and the long June evening was tiring at last, but it was still warm enough to sit in comfort without a coat, and Sheena always enjoyed this time of the day best. It was quiet and peaceful and the sand still retained enough of the warmth of the day, although it was growing more chill now as the sun lost its heat to the evening.

'I presume you mean Van Goalan,' she guessed, drawn

despite her reluctance to be disturbed, mainly by the subject of his remark, she admitted.

'I mean Cousin Van,' he agreed, then eyed her silently for a moment, his face curiously still, as it seldom was. 'You're swoony about him too, aren't you?' he asked at last.

'I – I admire him,' Sheena admitted, disliking the implication of schoolgirlish worship in his choice of phrase.

His rugged, almost droll, features grimaced apologetically. 'You admire him,' he allowed, 'and he admires you, though scarcely for the same reasons, of course.'

'No?' She was used to questioning his meaning and did so without hesitation. 'Why do you say that?'

'Why, for obvious reasons,' he insisted, adamant as always. 'He finds you attractive because you're a pretty—' He eyed her briefly. 'Correction, very beautiful girl, but *your* reasons must obviously be coloured by the fact that he's a very well-known and highly glamorized public figure.'

'You make me sound like a beastly little snob,' she accused, wondering uneasily how much truth there was in what he said.

'No, not a snob,' he denied blandly, 'just a normal, easily led female.'

That he was deliberately baiting her, she had no doubt, but she refused to rise to the bait, although she supposed she inevitably would sooner or later, as always. 'I'm sorry you have such a low opinion of the female sex,' she told him, sifting the yellow sand through the fingers of one hand.

'Oh, goodness, no, not me,' Gwyn denied earnestly. 'I love the little darlings, but it's because they're such a walkover, *en masse*, that people like Van can make a living out of the swoon business.'

'That's not fair at all,' Sheena declared. 'You've discounted altogether the fact that he's very talented, and you can't deny that.'

'Heaven forbid,' Gwyn vowed piously. 'He's a clever lad, I frankly admit it.'

'He's also a very attractive man,' Sheena insisted, 'though I don't suppose you've even considered that fact.'

'Indeed I have,' he admitted, 'but there are just as good-looking men about in the street, who aren't in the glamour business. Present company excepted, of course,' he added hastily, catching her meaningful look in his direction. 'You wouldn't even spare them more than a passing glance, I don't suppose, it's just because Van's got the added attraction of fame and glamour.'

'And you're the expert!' Sheena pouted her mouth and tipped her slightly retroussé nose at him disdainfully, a fact that seemed only to amuse him more.

'Don't look down your little pug nose at me, Tuppence,' he told her, unperturbed by the threatening storm. 'You know quite well what I mean and you know it makes sense. Not,' he added ruefully, 'that you'll ever admit it.'

'I shan't admit it,' Sheena told him, 'because it isn't true, and if you ask me, I think you're jealous of Van, just purely and simply jealous, because I said he's attractive.'

The inevitable denial took the form of a wry smile and one arched brow that spoke volumes. 'By saying I'm jealous because *you* find him attractive,' he pointed out, 'you're implying that I have designs on you myself. Now what gave you that idea?'

She turned on him indignantly, realizing too late how she had been led on to lose her temper, and her eyes betrayed her dismay when she saw the look in his. His burst of laughter tried her sorely, but she merely looked away again hastily and hugged her knees tight. 'I like Van,' she told him quietly, controlling her voice with difficulty. 'I like him because he's charming, good-looking and nice-mannered.'

Gwyn's face crinkled into the familiar grin. 'Then you should make a lovely pair,' he declared. 'With the exception of the last part, you're very alike.'

'I—' She looked at him, holding her tongue only with difficulty and bent on maintaining her dignity at all costs. Her soft mouth closed determinedly tight on the words that crowded her tongue.

'Spit it out, Tuppence,' he encouraged, 'or you'll burst.'

'I have no intention of doing anything so – so crude,' Sheena declared, her chin high.

'Dignity at all costs,' he teased. 'Good old Tuppence!'

It was not that she could not stand any more of his teasing, she was too used to it for that, but she felt the humour of the situation suddenly and was afraid she would spoil her dignified withdrawal by laughing, so she started to get to her feet with rather more haste than care.

Her legs were a little cramped with sitting so long hugging her knees and instead of gaining her feet, as she hoped, she lost her balance and toppled, falling across his knees. Her fall was halted by his arms that were round her so swiftly she had no chance to evade them and for a moment the breath was knocked out of her by the unexpectedness of it.

It was not a very dignified position, lying as she was across his lap, and she was close enough to the sun-browned face to distinguish the myriad tiny lines at the corners of his eyes and the glint of devilment that enjoyed her discomfiture.

'Whoops-a-daisy!' The facetious exclamation jolted her into action and she struggled to sit upright, hindered by the enfolding arms.

'Gwyn, help me up, you—'

'Aaah!' One brow cocked warningly and he held her for a second longer before pulling her, none too gently, off his knees and on to the sand beside him.

Sheena took a moment to recover herself, then scrambled to her feet, more successfully this time, brushing sand from her clothes with a vigorous hand and trying not to meet the eyes that still watched her. A brief, careless glance, however, and all her intentions went by the board in a burst of laughter.

Their disagreements never lasted very long, and she took it for granted when he stood up too, ready to accompany her. 'It's time I was getting back,' she said. 'Uncle John will think I've got myself lost.'

He grinned unbelievingly as they walked up the slight incline to the road. There was no promenade or sea wall at Lea Bay, only the wide, smooth stretch of beach, completely deserted, and neither of them spoke again until they reached Sheena's front garden, some seventy-five yards or so from the sea.

'Are we still sailing on Sunday?' Gwyn asked, brushing the persistent sand from his clothes as he stood with her by the gate.

'We arranged to, didn't we?' Sheena asked, and he nodded. 'Then we are, I suppose. Unless,' she added, 'you want to change your mind.'

He grinned at her knowingly. 'I rather thought *you* might,' he told her.

Sheena stood by the gatepost, one foot swinging, her eyes following its movement idly. 'I can't think why,' she said. 'I don't usually have last-minute changes of mind, do I?'

'Not usually,' he allowed with another grin, 'but then my cousin isn't usually around to make you have second thoughts.'

Sheena frowned at the top of the post, not looking at him. 'I don't quite see,' she said slowly, 'what your cousin's arrival has to do with my changing my mind about sailing with you. I don't flatter myself that he's that interested in me. You're just being facetious again, Gwyn, and I wish you wouldn't, not at my expense.'

No matter how firmly she had dismissed the idea of Van Goalan being interested in her to any extent, Sheena could not dismiss the thought of it entirely from her mind that he *had* been flatteringly attentive to her at their first meeting, and she turned hastily when he hailed her, only a couple of days later, as she passed the Madoc house.

He came hurrying down the last few yards of driveway to reach her, smiling in a way that set her heart doing crazy things. 'Are you going somewhere special?' he asked, after a preliminary greeting, and Sheena shook her head, a little uncertain of herself and of him. It was a little like talking to a dream, she thought, then promptly dismissed the idea as fanciful.

'Not really anywhere special,' she told him, 'I'm just walking.'

'Then may I join you?' He fell into step beside her and she nodded, feeling unusually tongue-tied. 'You have no particular object in view?' he asked.

'Not exactly,' Sheena smiled uncertainly, 'although I had thought of going as far as Lea Point. I'm thinking of doing a painting of it and I like to sit and ponder for a bit first.'

'Oh yes, of course, you're a painter.' The gleaming white smile encompassed her again and once more set her mind racing off in all directions at once. 'I've heard great things about you from Gwyn and Uncle George.'

'Oh, they're – well, prejudiced in my favour, I suppose,' she demurred, but he shook his head firmly in denial.

'I have to admit to knowing very little about these things,' he confessed with a smile, 'because I have so little time to spare, but I hear you've been very successful with your work.'

Sheena wished she was not so embarrassingly conscious of his attraction, illogically blaming Gwyn and his remarks for the way she felt. 'I've been very lucky,' she allowed, 'and everyone's been very kind.'

'Deservedly so if that lovely view of the bay is yours,' he told her. 'The one in the dining-room; it's beautiful and very well done.' He laughed apologetically. 'Please don't take that to be as patronizing as it sounded,' he begged.

'It didn't sound in the least patronizing,' Sheena denied, feeling the colour in her cheeks at his praise of her work. 'I'm delighted you like it. I painted it for Uncle George's birthday last year and I'm afraid he makes rather a lot of it.'

'No more than it deserves,' he told her. 'I like it enormously.' The blue eyes sought hers, one hand slipping lightly round her arm as they walked. 'Will you paint one for me when you have time, Sheena? I'll pay for it, of course, you *are* a professional painter, after all.'

Rather overcome by the suddenness of it, Sheena nodded. 'I'll – I'll do one with pleasure,' she said. 'I'd like to give it to you, though, as a – a sort of token.' She felt a little light-headed at the sudden air of intimacy in their conversation and sounded rather breathless, realizing too late the impression she had probably given.

He cocked an eyebrow at her in fair imitation of Gwyn, a half smile recognizing her motive. 'I'd much rather you

23

didn't,' he said. 'It's very sweet of you, but you see – well, the truth is that a lot of girls send me things as tokens, and I don't want to think of you as just another fan, Sheena.'

'Oh – I'm sorry.' She felt doubly embarrassed because she had not only been impulsive but also undoubtedly rather naïve and schoolgirlish as well.

'Please don't be sorry.' The hand on her arm tightened reassuringly and there was only friendly concern for her embarrassment in his eyes when she glanced up at him. 'It was very sweet of you to offer to give it to me, but I should feel almost as if I'd—' He shrugged in that vaguely foreign way that was so attractive. 'As if I'd asked you for it,' he added, 'so let me – commission? – the painting. Your talent is sufficient for it to be discounted as a mere gesture on my part.'

Sheena considered the idea for a moment, then turned her dark eyes and smiled at him. 'I perhaps didn't word it very well the first time,' she admitted, 'but please, if you'll let me, I'd like to give it to you as a – a friend, perhaps for your birthday, as I did Uncle George. Will you let me do that?'

'I'd be enchanted, thank you.' She was glad his thanks were not too effusive or she would have felt them less sincere, and his sincerity, she felt, was as much part of his charm as the good looks and a hundred and one other things that made up the almost hypnotic personality that was Van Goalan.

She smiled to herself as she walked along the sea road with him and considered how many women would have given a right arm to have been in her place – having his whole attention and his arm tucked cosily through hers as they walked.

'Do you know Lea Point?' She felt bound to make conversation since silence gave her time to think and her thoughts kept straying off at the most unlikely tangents.

He laughed and made a grimace of regret. 'I'm afraid I don't know this part of the world at all,' he confessed. 'It seems a delightful little place, what I've seen of it so far, and not at all as I expected.'

Sheena smiled understanding. 'You expected something like Sandlea?' she guessed, and his smile admitted it. 'This is quite different, we don't get any visitors here, not holidaymakers, that is, and we don't really encourage them, I have to admit.'

'The holidaymaker is my bread and butter,' he told her, only mildly reproachful, 'you mustn't malign him.'

'Oh, I wasn't maligning them,' Sheena protested, 'please don't think that, it's just that – well, we don't really relish the idea of hot-dog stands under the trees.' She laughed apologetically. 'Gwyn says I'm a snob and you probably agree with him, but I'm not really, we just prefer to keep our little community the way we like it. After all, we chose to live here all year round, not just a couple of weeks in a year.'

'You like it here?' It was more statement than question, and Sheena nodded.

'It's been my home for the last fifteen years. I love it.'

'Have you known Gwyn that long?' It was Gwyn he named, she noticed, not his father or the two of them together, and his reason puzzled her momentarily.

'Not quite,' she said. 'Uncle George and Gwyn moved here about twelve years ago.'

'Oh, I see.' He sounded as if her answer explained something to him, although she could not imagine what.

'That's Lea Point,' she informed him as they left the road and walked down the beach.

He followed her pointing finger and looked at the long

curving peninsula of bare sand that made the bay appear even deeper, and stood only slightly higher than the surrounding beach. Only a rounded promontory at the very end of it distinguished it as other than a ridge in the sand, and that rose some nine or ten feet above the lapping tide.

'Is it covered at high tide?' he asked, and Sheena shook her head.

'Only about two thirds of it, the strip that runs from the tip to the mainland, or the main beach, I should say. Strictly speaking, I suppose, it's an island, though no one ever refers to it as one.'

He eyed the mound of glistening yellow sand in the bright sunlight and smiled. 'How romantic, your own desert island.'

'It may look like a desert island to you at the moment,' Sheena remarked, 'but when it's wet and blowy it can be more like the Antarctic, and I should know. Gwyn once stranded me there on a cold wet day and I felt like an iceberg.'

He looked quite shocked at the idea. 'What on earth possessed him?' he asked, and Sheena wondered if he was as horrified as he looked.

'The devil, I suspect,' she quipped, laughing now at the incident that had infuriated her at the time. 'Gwyn's full of tricks like that when he considers I need taking down a peg or two.'

'Oh, but how could he?' he protested, evidently taking the whole thing much more seriously than she had intended. 'How long were you there?'

'Oh, only about twenty minutes or so.' She shrugged, making light of the episode. 'His conscience bothered him and he came back for me. He always does,' she admitted with a smile.

He gave a rather theatrical shudder as they neared the

strip of sand that formed the approach to the point and glanced at the shimmering water only feet away. 'It's as well to know the lie of the land, it seems to me,' he declared, 'otherwise one could be in trouble.'

'It is a fairly tricky part of the coast, I suppose,' Sheena admitted, 'but it's safe enough if you know it.'

'Is Sandlea like this?' he asked, and she shook her head.

'No, that's safe enough.' She glanced up at him from under her lashes. 'But you won't be able to use that beach, will you? You'd get mobbed by your fans.'

He pulled a wry face. 'True enough,' he said. 'I'll have to rely on you to keep me out of trouble while I'm here.'

Sheena felt shy again suddenly, possibly because the conversation had once again become more personal and intimate. 'I'll do anything I can to help, of course,' she agreed, 'but Gwyn knows as much of the lie of the land as I do, and he's on the spot for you.'

The blue eyes held hers for a long moment and she felt her heart racing again. 'Gwyn's out all day when I need a guide,' he told her, 'apart from the fact that he might take it into his head to dump me ashore at high tide and leave me there as he did you. Besides,' he added with a smile lighting his good-looking face, 'you're *much* prettier than Gwyn.'

27

CHAPTER TWO

ALTHOUGH it had been rather dull the last few days, Sunday morning was bright and sunny again and Sheena opened her eyes to shafts of bright sunlight shimmering across her bedroom walls, and a warm summer breeze blowing the curtains, like colourful sails, into the room.

Today she was going to Barbell Sands with Van and it just had to be a lovely day. Nothing could spoil the glow of anticipation she felt at the prospect of spending a whole day with the most exciting man she had ever known. Not even some small, niggling doubt at the back of her mind that she could neither identify nor dismiss.

The invitation to spend the day with him had been not exactly unexpected, but still exciting for all that, and Van had promised to bring a picnic lunch so that they could spend the whole day doing nothing but laze and swim. It was much safer swimming from Barbell Sands and still had the necessary advantage of isolation so that Van need have no fear of being recognized and their day spoiled by clamouring admirers.

She stretched lazily and mentally ran through her available wardrobe for something suitable to wear. Something not too exotic to look out of place on a beach picnic, but not so utilitarian as to be unattractive. She decided eventually on a green linen suit, which had shorts and a top that would pass muster as a dress and under which she could easily wear a swim suit. That shade of green suited her very well, even Gwyn admitted that. She smiled to herself at the thought of Gwyn, then a second later sat bolt upright in bed, her pleasurable anticipation vanished in the sudden and awful realization of what she had done.

No wonder she had been troubled by some indefinable worry at the back of her mind! She remembered walking up from the beach with Gwyn on Monday evening and his reminder that they were going sailing the following Sunday – today. She had been rather superior, she seemed to remember, telling him that she was not given to sudden changes of mind, and he had made some half amused reference to his cousin's unaccustomed presence and its possible effect on her. Now she had done exactly as he had implied she would.

Instinctively she sought to transfer the blame and told herself that surely Van would have mentioned that he was taking her on a picnic today, so Gwyn had had plenty of time to point out to her and his cousin that she had a prior arrangement with him. Unless, as was possible with Gwyn, he had deliberately allowed the matter to drift with the intention of seeing what she would do.

Suddenly the prospect of the day she had anticipated so joyfully seemed less enjoyable and she could only think of Gwyn's possible reaction when she told him of her forgetfulness, if he did not already know. It did not for a moment occur to her to consider telling Van she had a previous arrangement with his cousin; it would have to be Gwyn who took a back seat, and she sighed at the prospect of telling him so.

She dressed slowly, in no hurry to discover what reaction she would get, and she caught her uncle's curious eye on her at breakfast. 'Not feeling well?' he asked.

'Oh yes, I'm fine, thanks.' She sighed in sympathy with herself and John Cameron half-smiled.

'You look and sound as if you have all the troubles in the world on your shoulders,' he told her. 'Can I help?'

'Not really,' she admitted, 'unless you'd care to tell

Gwyn that I've arranged to spend the day with Van Goalan and I'd clean forgotten about going sailing with him.'

'Oh dear!' Her uncle eyed her ruefully. 'If Gwyn had first call, you know, he should get priority. Do I gather you were thinking along opposite lines?'

Sheena looked not only unhappy but a little defiant as she stirred sugar into her coffee. 'I'd much rather go with Van, and he *is* a visitor after all. It wouldn't be very good-mannered to let him down at such short notice.'

'It wouldn't be very good manners to do it to Gwyn either,' her uncle declared, 'but I don't suppose that's quite the same, is it?'

'Well, it *isn't*,' Sheena insisted, on the defensive. 'Van only has Sundays free.'

'So does Gwyn,' he countered, 'or at least Saturday's a free day as well, I suppose, even if he does sometimes go in for half an hour.'

'Oh, it's not the same,' Sheena insisted. 'Gwyn's – well, he's used to me and I don't suppose he'll mind all that much; after all, he only takes me because there's no one else available.'

'Oh, I don't think that's quite fair, is it, sweetheart?' John Cameron eyed her pretty, half-defiant face for a moment.

'Well, maybe not,' Sheena allowed at last, reluctantly, 'but I can't let Van down, Uncle John, I just can't. Gwyn will – will understand, I'm sure he will.'

'I'm sure he will,' her uncle agreed wryly. 'Poor old Gwyn!'

'He's not poor old Gwyn,' Sheena denied, her conscience prickling uneasily, 'and please don't make me feel any more guilty than I already do about it. He'll get over it, if it bothers him at all.'

'Old faithful,' her uncle quoted. 'You know you accused

me of treating Suna badly the other day,' he reminded her, 'but you're just as bad when it comes to Gwyn, in fact you're worse, because so far I've never made a date with Suna and with someone else at the same time.'

'I didn't say you treated her badly,' Sheena denied. 'I said you neglected her shamefully, and anyway it's not the same thing at all. Gwyn isn't in love.'

Her uncle's handsome face looked mildly startled for a moment. 'Meaning that Suna is?' he asked quietly, and Sheena lowered her gaze, fearing she had become too personal, although she felt sure he must know by now how Suna felt about him.

'It's none of my business, I suppose,' she admitted, 'but – well, I thought you and Suna—'

'Me and Suna?' He smiled wryly. 'You're trying your hand at match-making now, are you? Well, from what I can see, my girl, you'd better get your own tangles sorted out before you start on mine, eh?'

Sheena sighed, her own problem taking precedence again. 'Oh, Uncle John, what on earth am I going to do?'

'Ring up Gwyn?' he suggested, and she grimaced ruefully.

'I suppose so,' she agreed, 'though heaven knows what he'll say when he knows. He's always so – so condescending about Van, and he's bound to crow over me because I've made a mess of things. He'll never let me live it down, I know him.'

'I don't think he'll be as bad as all that,' her uncle denied, 'and there's not much else you can do, is there?'

Sheena sighed again as she got up from the table, her coffee only half gone and rapidly getting cold. 'No, I suppose not,' she said.

Far from sounding upset at the news of her mistake Gwyn, when he came to the telephone, sounded quite happy. 'Not to worry,' he told her blithely, and something in his manner made her suspicious. It was not like Gwyn to let her get off so lightly.

'Did – did you know?'

'Not until this morning,' he told her, 'when I heard Van inquiring after a picnic lunch for two, then I asked who the lucky girl was and discovered it was you.'

'You're not – not angry about it?'

'Angry? Bless you, my child, I know you well enough by now. I anticipated being stood up by you, Tuppence, and I've already organized myself another dolly.'

'Oh – oh, I see.' Her feelings were evident in the tone of her voice and she heard him chuckle.

'Sauce for the goose, my girl,' he told her, obviously enjoying the situation, so that Sheena wondered what else he had up his sleeve that he had not yet told her. With Gwyn she never quite knew what to expect. Used to the machinations of big business, he enjoyed nothing better than a challenge to his ingenuity and he could, on occasion, be as devious as anyone she knew.

'You're sure you don't mind?' His easy acceptance was just not in character, and it worried her.

'No, of course not. I told you, I'm nicely suited elsewhere, thank you.'

Sheena was silent for a moment, still uncertain. 'Why did you anticipate I wouldn't be coming with you?' she asked, and realized a moment later that she could have supplied the answer to that herself.

'Easy,' he told her, 'mostly your blind adoration of Cousin Van and Van's penchant for beautiful girls. And,' he added with a chuckle, 'a pretty sound knowledge of you, my girl.'

'I see.' She drew a deep breath. 'Well, I'm sorry, Gwyn.'

There seemed little else to say, although he sounded far

less bothered by her *faux pas* than she did. 'All's well that ends well,' he quoted, 'and I'm sure we'll have just as much fun with four of us.'

'Four of us?' Suspicion edged her voice again and she could already feel the resentment stirring in her. 'I don't understand, Gwyn.'

'Oh, don't you?' he said airily. 'I thought perhaps Van might have rung you and told you of the new arrangements, but perhaps *he* didn't bother either.'

'What new arrangements?'

'Cora and I are joining your beach picnic.'

'Oh, I see.'

'Tuppence, that's three times you've used that phrase in the last few minutes,' he told her, his tone mildly disapproving. 'You really should try and widen your vocabulary.'

'Oh, don't try to be funny,' Sheena said crossly. 'I'm sorry I made a mess of things, but that doesn't give you the right to be sarcastic at my expense. Who *is* Cora?' she added a second later, and he made no secret of his amusement, the sound of his laughter tickling her ear against the receiver.

'Who is Cora, what is she – ee,' he sang, sadly off tune, and laughed again. 'Cora, my delectable Tuppence, is the siren of our secretarial pool and a very desirable property.'

'I see.' She realized too late that she had used the same phrase yet again and she heard him tut-tut admonishment. 'Oh, stop it!' she cried. 'I have a right to know who's invading my beach picnic. I was looking forward to it.'

'*We* still are,' Gwyn told her. 'Cora's another fan of my swoony cousin too, so you'll have to face some competition, I'm afraid, Tuppence. Not that she can match you in the beauty stakes, but she's a nice girl and not at all gooey-eyed about it.'

Sheena ignored the implication of that. 'Van was picking me up here at eleven,' she said. 'Is he still coming?'

'Of course, only he'll have company, that's all. We're using my transport, incidentally, there's more room for four than in Van's little wagon, though it's not quite so cosy, I suppose.'

Sheena sighed resignedly. 'All right, I'll expect you about eleven – all of you.' She made a grimace of disappointment as she put down the receiver, her eyes thoughtful.

She was horribly disappointed and rather sorry for herself and she would make no secret of it, although she supposed she had been lucky that Gwyn had taken it as he had. The main thing she disliked about the new arrangement, she had to admit, was the addition of the mysterious Cora to the party. She had been so looking forward to having Van to herself and now she would be obliged to share him with another, equally ardent admirer, while Gwyn, no doubt, would sit back and enjoy the situation, knowing she had brought it on herself.

'Bother Gwyn!' she muttered crossly as she glared at the silent telephone. Her uncle's amusement when she told him about the new arrangement did nothing to appease her self-righteous indignation at having her plans spoiled.

It was a little before eleven when Gwyn's car drew up in front of the house, its horn summoning her stridently, and she went out to answer it, openly curious about the newcomer to the party. It was Van who got out and saw her into the back seat with him, and Gwyn who introduced the girl beside him in the front.

'Cora, meet Sheena Hastings, an old friend of mine. Sheena, this is Cora Lindsey, also an old friend. I met her when I was climbing the ladder and we've been friends ever since.'

Cora Lindsey turned her head, more uncertain than her rather cool manner implied, Sheena thought, and rather older than she had expected. She must have been about Gwyn's age, but the thirty years or so sat on her lightly and she had an air of freshness about her that was refreshing. She was, Sheena recognized, more attractive than pretty, with short brown hair that was not quite straight and rather nice grey eyes that were smiling at Sheena over the back of the seat.

'Hello, Miss Hastings.' A slim hand was proffered briefly and Sheena took it with an uncertain smile.

'Miss Lindsey.'

'Before we go any further,' Gwyn declared in what Sheena always called his bossy voice, 'we'll have less formality for a start. Miss Hastings and Miss Lindsey sound idiotic on a beach picnic. Make it Sheena and Cora and we'll start.'

The two girls exchanged glances, both of them, it seemed to Sheena, quite accustomed to Gwyn's ways, and they smiled wryly at one another. 'Hello, Sheena.'

Sheena acknowledged the inevitability of it with a grimace at Gwyn's back. 'Hello, Cora.'

'Now, you obstinate Welshman,' Cora told him with an easy familiarity that took Sheena by surprise, 'we'll start, if you're satisfied.'

The air of comradeship between them gave Sheena food for thought as they started off along the sea road, and it made her more quiet than even her annoyance at having her outing invaded would have done. She wondered why she had never heard Gwyn mention the other woman, since he seemed to know her so well and had done for a long time, apparently. He had referred to the time when he was climbing the ladder, in other words while he was still learning the business from the bottom

35

upwards, and that had been twelve years now, as long as he had known Sheena herself. For some reason she found the knowledge discomfiting.

The drive to Barbell Sands took about ten minutes and was along an open road with the wide green expanse of common land on one side and quiet stretches of sandy beach on the other. With the top of the car open it was delightfully cool and refreshing and a ride which Sheena had enjoyed often before.

Sheena's long dark hair, however, weathered the welcome breeze rather less well than Cora's much shorter style and Gwyn grinned as he glanced at her in the mirror briefly. 'You'll look like a bonfire when we arrive,' he told her. 'You should have tied your locks back.'

'Thank you for the compliment.' Sheena glared at the back of his head, remembering all the times he had assured her that she looked quite presentable with her hair tumbled and tossed as it was now.

'Actually it looks rather attractive like that,' Van told her, his eyes consoling her for his cousin's lack of tact.

Sheena smiled, putting her hands to the mass of dark hair that gave her a rather gypsy look, definitely intriguing. 'I should have known better than to drive with Gwyn without having every hair firmly anchored,' she admitted. 'He gets delusions of grandeur when he's behind a wheel and thinks he's at Silverstone.' Gwyn allowed the jibe with no more than an amiable grin at her reflection and Sheena, seeing her efforts wasted, pulled back her hair with one hand. 'Oh well, it's too late now, I'll do something about it when we stop.'

Barbell Sands was as isolated as it was possible to be. The road they were travelling on veered off some fifty or sixty yards before the sands started and left them virtually hidden from view of all but the most determined explorer. Following the road, few people ever discovered their existence, but it had been a favourite place of Sheena's ever since she was a little girl, and there was something special about it to her, some air of unreality that never failed to affect her.

Long, coarse grass grew along the ridge of the dunes that backed the beach, waving and sighing in the permanent wind. A wide sweep of golden brown sand eased gently down to the sea, offering a sense of freedom and no distractions, for as far as the eye could see there was nothing but sand and sea and the shimmering haze of distance that looked as if it disappeared over the edge of the world.

Van looked at Sheena, some expression in his eyes that shared her disappointment at not being there alone. 'It looks a wonderful place,' he said for her ears alone. 'We must come here again.'

Sheena nodded, aware that Gwyn was watching them, a glint of humour in his eyes as if he knew exactly how they felt. 'We have to walk from here,' he informed his cousin. 'The springs start objecting if you take them too far over this bumpy ground and it gets worse as it gets nearer the dunes. Anyway, it's not very far to walk.'

An ever-widening expanse of common land ran between them and the road as they walked towards the sea and added to the sense of isolation. With only the sea and the light wind audible it gave one a slightly eerie feeling at first and even footsteps were deadened on the turf and sand, only voices carrying a remarkably long way.

Sheena had visited it so often with Gwyn that she glanced at him almost involuntarily as she walked beside Van, down over the dunes. The wink he gave her in response did nothing to still the vague sense of uneasiness she tried hard to dismiss.

Cora confessed to never having been there before and, for some reason, the information cheered Sheena, although she had no idea why, except that possibly it made her less at home there than Sheena was.

'It's a wonderful spot,' Cora said, curling up on the rug that had been spread on the sand and smiling at Gwyn who sat beside her, 'it's so beautifully quiet and still.'

Van nodded understanding, looking round at the whispering grasses on the top of the dunes, bending in the light breeze and at the glittering expanse of sea. 'It is wonderful,' he agreed, 'and so full of – of feeling.' His expressive actor's face showed him genuinely moved by his surroundings. 'It's almost – primitive, glorious in its simplicity.'

'Oh, very poetic!' Gwyn teased him, although the look of understanding in his own eyes showed that he shared the emotions stirred by their surroundings.

'That's what I meant exactly,' Cora sighed, 'only I couldn't put it into the right words. It has a feeling of endlessness as if it has never changed.'

'Your turn, Tuppence,' Gwyn encouraged, the inevitable grin inviting her to express her feelings, if she dared. 'Does it arouse your primitive instincts too?'

Sheena as always was affected by the atmosphere of the place, but she refused to be teased about it and lifted her chin at him haughtily. 'I might in some circumstances,' she admitted, leaving no doubt as to her meaning. 'And don't call me that.'

'Tuppence?' It was Van who took up the remark, his expression curious, trying to placate her. 'It's rather delightful, and very apt in view of your big dark eyes.'

Sheena turned the big dark eyes in question and smiled at him, sensing Gwyn's sudden change of expression. 'I've got a copyright on it,' he warned his cousin. 'I invented it.'

Van smiled, a smile that spoke volumes and set Sheena's heart and mind racing wildly in every conceivable direction. 'Sheena is much prettier,' he told her, his voice lowered as he leaned ever so slightly nearer to her, 'and therefore more appropriate. It's Scottish, isn't it?'

Sheena smiled and lowered her eyes, wishing Gwyn and Cora Lindsey miles away. She felt so horribly gauche and vulnerable sitting there on that open beach with Gwyn's eyes watching her so speculatively, and with Cora trying hard to look as if she wasn't there.

'Oh aye, she's a hard-headed Scot,' Gwyn laughed, forestalling her answer, with an atrociously exaggerated accent, and raising an old familiar, though usually good-humoured argument.

'I'm Scots on my mother's side,' Sheena said, ignoring the attempt to rouse her to argument.

'Of course, yes, your uncle's name should have told me that.' The blue eyes held hers steadily and she found it difficult to look away again. 'But I *can* see Gwyn's reason for calling you Tuppence.' He somehow managed to convey a compliment with the words and Sheena felt her heart skip crazily.

'It's a name I grew out of years ago,' she said, 'only Gwyn will persist in it. Just to be difficult mostly, I think.' She lifted her chin as she voiced the accusation and looked at her tormentor, and the way she wrinkled her nose at him was perhaps more instinctive than conscious.

'Are you dressed for swimming?' he asked, laughing softly in a way that made her bite her lip when she realized the reason for it.

'Of course, aren't we all?' She looked at Van, who nodded agreement.

'Well, I'm going to take the plunge,' Gwyn declared, already stripping off his shirt. 'When we come out, the girls can use the car and we can go native here. Are you coming in, Van?'

It was only minutes before they were all four ready for the water and Sheena trying not to notice how much more bronzed and fit Gwyn looked beside his paler cousin. She was rather surprised to see Cora in a very demure one-piece costume in dark blue, which contrasted very markedly with her own brief yellow bikini that looked brighter coloured than ever against her bronzed skin.

She piled her long dark hair under a cap and was aware of Van's eyes watching her with an expression that brought a flush of colour to her cheeks. 'You look very beautiful,' he told her, *sotto voce*, as they went down to the water, and she smiled, incredibly shy suddenly although she had worn this same costume several times before and even borne Gwyn's not always tactful remarks on its brevity.

The water, as often was the case at this time of the year, was colder than one expected and the girls' voices shivered through the quiet as they took the plunge, the men more stoically silent. Van proved an excellent swimmer and Sheena could not help wondering when he found the time to practise, voicing her curiosity when he trod water beside her, taking a breather.

'My own pool,' he informed her, and she nodded understanding when he looked slightly apologetic about it. 'It's the only way I can have a swim in peace, although I don't get much time these days.'

'Of course,' she said, paddling lazily beside him, 'it must be difficult for you to do lots of things that most of us take for granted.'

A wry smile acknowledged it, but at the same time dismissed any suggestion of regret. 'There are far more advantages than disadvantages,' he told her, and smiled in such a way that she shook water from her eyes to hide the quick flush of colour to her face.

With his blond hair clinging wetly to his head, he looked darker and somehow more aggressively masculine than usual, more like Gwyn, she realized with a start, and shook her head to rid herself of the comparison, while the blue eyes regarded her with interest and speculation. 'We'll come here again,' he told her, as quietly as it was possible with the water lapping round them, 'just the two of us, Sheena. I'm sorry about today, with things as they were. There wasn't much I could do about it except agree to Gwyn's suggestion that he and his lady came too.'

Sheena made a wry face over her own mistake. 'It was my fault,' she said. 'I clean forgot I'd promised to go sailing with Gwyn.'

She saw the blue eyes glow warmly and the good-looking face, shiny with sea water and suddenly less boyish, lean towards her. His mouth covered hers, warm and tasting of salt, and she closed her eyes, only to flick them open in panic a second later when something tugged at her ankles and pulled her downwards under the water, while she fought for breath.

Only a couple of feet away as she went down, she saw Gwyn's brown face wearing its inevitable grin and distorted by the shimmering water, his thick hair spread out round his head like a separate living creature as he swam lazily, waiting for her reaction. It was not the first time he had done that, in fact it was quite usual when they went swimming and normally she did no more than make an effort at revenge, although it was usually useless, for he was like an eel in the water.

This time was different, however, for not only had she not been expecting it but she was furious with him for choosing that particular moment to duck her. She broke the surface, shaking her head angrily to clear her eyes, and saw Van some five or six yards away looking round for her. 'Sheena!' He raised a hand when he spotted her yellow cap and started towards her, while Sheena trod water, recovering her breath.

A swift dark shape just below her warned her this time and she started towards Van, her body cleaving the water as fast as her arms and legs would take her, but not fast enough to evade the hands that reached for her and pulled her down again. She struggled and hit out wildly, both useless in the water, as she would have realized at any other time.

'Gwyn!' Her anger exploded as they both shot to the surface and he submerged again just in time to avoid the wildly aimed blow to his face, his grin still in evidence and wearing a look of satisfaction that infuriated her.

Even though he did not bother her again, the intimacy of the brief moment with Van was impossible to recover and she was in no good humour when finally they came out of the water, leaving Gwyn and Cora still swimming.

'I'm sorry,' Van said, rightly interpreting her expression as they walked up the beach to where they had left their things.

'*You* don't have to apologize,' Sheena told him, releasing her long hair from the cap and shaking it loose round her shoulders. 'I'll deal with Gwyn later!'

There was an almost childish ring to the threat and Van smiled as he looked down at the soft mouth pouted crossly and the angry sparkle in her dark eyes. 'Maybe I should warn him,' he suggested lightly. 'You sound as if you intend being violent.'

'One of these days—' She swung the wet cap hard to shake off the water, leaving the rest of the threat unspoken.

They walked slowly up the sandy stretch and it was almost as if the tranquillizing effect of the place worked on her as they went, so that she felt a lot less angry by the time they reached their chosen spot, although there was still a niggle of resentment against Gwyn, deep inside her.

It was silly of her, she supposed, to let him get under her skin the way he did and she must try and treat him less as if his behaviour mattered to her. After all, she was here with Van and nothing he did could change that; all his sly changing of plans could not alter the fact that she was with Van as *his* girl, not Gwyn's. It was a lovely day and there was no reason why she should not enjoy herself as she had intended. 'I refuse to be ruffled,' she told Van with a rueful smile, 'because that's what he wants, but it's a beautiful day and I mean to make the most of it.'

'Wise girl!' For a second she thought she detected a hint of Gwyn's rather patronizing manner in the comment, but the way the blue eyes glowed warmly at her banished the idea, and she reached for the huge towel she always used on the beach, her cheeks warmly flushed as she bent her head.

She had barely time to rub off the surplus moisture when Gwyn and Cora joined them and her resentment rekindled momentarily when she glared at Gwyn almost unconsciously.

'What have I done?' he asked plaintively, although his eyes betrayed his knowledge only too well, and Sheena rubbed the towel vigorously over her shoulders, not deigning to answer.

Always, ever since she was a child, she had had difficulty in reaching round to dry her *own* back after she had been swimming, and from habit he took the towel from her and moved round behind her.

'Don't!' The one word, short and sharp, startled Van as much as it did Gwyn and he looked from one to the other curiously.

'Have I got the sack?' When Gwyn spoke as quietly as that it was a sign that he was either angry or hurt, and Sheena was unsure which it was now, but she took the towel from him and tried to ignore the small, cold silence that waited for her answer.

'I can manage – thank you.'

For a moment she thought he might argue, perhaps be as scathingly sarcastic as only he could be, but he simply watched her for a moment in silence, then shrugged, as if it mattered little one way or the other. 'Suit yourself, Tuppence. Maybe after twelve years you *can* manage – I'm sorry.'

She glanced up hastily, touched by the reproach more than she cared to admit, but he was already busy with his own towel, scrubbing away at the brown body as if he was taking revenge on something he hated. The hand she had partly raised to touch his arm in a gesture of appeal dropped slowly, its consolation rebuffed.

'I don't know about anyone else,' Cora said suddenly, breaking the uneasy silence, 'but I'm famished.' Sheena was grateful for her intervention and looked across at her, surprising a smile that understood both her anger and her regret. She would, Sheena thought, like Cora Lindsey after all.

It was as well that George Madoc's housekeeper had been generous with the picnic, for their appetites were sharpened by the swim and they set to with a will after the girls had made an attractive spread on the two rugs covering the sand.

'Your Mrs. Groome must be a real treasure,' Cora told Gwyn as she eyed the variety of food. 'This is a wonderful spread.'

'It always is,' Gwyn told her with a grin, 'and she knows what Sheena and I like.' The last was accompanied by a swift, lightly intimate glance at Sheena and, to her

44

horror, she felt her cheeks colour warmly.

She looked hastily at Van to see if he had witnessed her unaccustomed sensitivity. She had never before blushed at anything Gwyn said, except in anger, and she hoped that if Van had noticed it would not be misinterpreted. If he had noticed, however, he gave no sign, and she was left to puzzle over her own uncharacteristic reaction.

No one felt like doing anything except laze in the sun after the huge lunch they had eaten and they were all four stretched out on the rugs more than half asleep, it seemed. They were well above the tide line and had no worries on that score, although the waves flipped and rippled only a few feet away, a slow, sighing accompaniment to lethargy that almost shushed Sheena to sleep.

Through half-closed lids she could just see Van's length stretched out beside her and sensed his hand inching towards her seconds before his fingers curled over hers. Lifting incredibly heavy eyelids, she looked at him and smiled, meeting some expression in his eyes that both puzzled and excited her.

'Let's walk.' No sound accompanied the mouthed words and she turned her head instinctively to look at Gwyn and Cora, both equally lazy, their faces turned towards one another, a fact which for some reason she could not name made Sheena hesitate.

After a moment, however, she nodded agreement and sat up, trying to make as little sound as possible. Van was already on his feet and offered a hand to help her rise, his good-looking face showing every sign of satisfaction at her compliance.

'Have fun!' Gwyn's deep voice, edged with laughter, halted Sheena as she started to walk away and she looked back. Down at the rugged brown face and the depth of laughter in his eyes, laughter and something else that held her for a moment uncertainly before she turned

45

away without answering.

Before they had taken more than a couple of steps, however, the wordless silence was suddenly disturbed by the babble and chatter of many voices growing louder every second. Sheena looked across the expanse of common land, her eyes registering dismay at the sight of a gaily clad party of holidaymakers, straggling over the turf like confetti on a lawn, and heading in their direction as if guided by some communal instinct.

'Visitors.' Gwyn raised a lazy head and Sheena could have sworn that the smile that crooked his mouth had a look of satisfaction about it.

The indistinguishable babble of sound was already beginning to take the form of words and the ones most easily recognizable were 'Van Goalan' and 'it's him!' The speed of approach of the colourful procession was already increasing, making Van's retreat impossible, since there was nowhere for him to go and nothing but the endless reaches of sand and sea stretching to infinity. Sheena felt her fingers curl and the sudden bitter taste of panic as she clung to his hand tightly, wondering how anyone could willingly face such a crowd as Van must have done often.

His sigh was possibly more resigned than regretful and Sheena was reminded that he had reproached her once for being uncharitable about holidaymakers. They were his bread-and-butter, he had said, and she supposed he was right, they were, and as such were to be not only tolerated but encouraged. It was a feeling she could not, at this moment, share and she shook her head in dismay.

'Comes of having a celebrity in the family,' Gwyn declared matter-of-factly, grinning as he sat up and hugged his knees. 'Walk over and greet 'em, will you, Van, then the rest of us won't get trampled underfoot by your en-

46

thusiastic admirers!'

Van's hesitation was brief. He ran careful hands over his smooth head and adjusted the open collar of his shirt to a more rakish stance, then walked with practised grace and confidence to meet the advancing party.

'Marvellous, isn't it?' Gwyn asked with a grin, but what sounded like genuine admiration for his cousin's bearing. 'Instant charm.'

'I'd be scared to death to face them,' Sheena admitted, watching the crowd surrounding Van, who was now almost invisible among them.

Once they had their quarry the rest of the party ceased to have any interest for the surging, eager gabble of sound and colour, and Sheena sat down again, rather disconsolately. 'Never mind,' Gwyn told her, in a tone that seemed to her more taunt than consolation, 'perhaps you just weren't meant to walk off into the romantic distance with my handsome cousin.'

Sheena looked at him, reproachful and suddenly suspicious. 'How on earth did they know he'd be here of all places?' she puzzled. 'It's not as if it's an easy place to find – in fact it's so remote from the road it's highly unlikely that a coach would find it without previous knowledge. They never come this far off the road.'

Gwyn shrugged, his chin resting on the arms that hugged his knees, his eyes speculative and still amused. 'Coincidence?' he suggested, while Cora eyed him a little doubtfully.

'I suppose someone could have tipped off the coach driver,' she guessed. 'Some of the more fervent fans would go anywhere to get a glimpse of their favourite celebrity, I know, and as Sheena says, this isn't the most easy place in the world to find.'

'Why would the coach driver leave the road at all?' Sheena asked, taking up the argument again. 'I've never known one come here before, and there's nothing to indicate that the sands are here, no signposts or notices. From the road it just looks like open common land with a glimpse of the sea in the distance. There must have been some reason for the driver to leave his normal route and drive down here.'

'Someone who likes Van, an admirer who heard a whisper and told the others,' Cora guessed, but Sheena shook her head, watching Gwyn as he gazed out at the endless sea, glittering in the sun, a faint smile still touching his mouth.

'Or someone who's jealous of him,' she suggested quietly, and held his gaze challengingly when he turned his head and looked at her. 'Someone who wanted to spoil his day.'

Gwyn looked across at the fair-haired figure busily signing autographs, his good-looking face alight with smiles as he spoke to each one in turn. 'I don't think Van would agree with you that his day's been spoiled,' he told her. 'He's enjoying himself, it's the breath of life to him.' He turned and looked at her quizzically and not without sympathy. 'Whether you like it or not, Tuppence,' he added softly, 'that's his world.'

CHAPTER THREE

THE niggling suspicion that Gwyn had somehow been responsible for the arrival of the coach party at Barbell Sands persisted and, although it was always at the back of Sheena's mind, she had never yet tackled him with it. For one thing she faced the fact that she had a strange reluctance to learn the truth in case it should prove him responsible.

She was forced to admit that, fond as he was of teasing her, he had never so far done anything deliberately spiteful, and she was pretty certain he would not be sufficiently bent on paying her back for her mix up over the dates to do such a thing to Van.

She saw a lot of Van during the days that followed for, although he was sometimes busy with the business side of his career, he was mostly free in the mornings and when he was he spent most of the time with Sheena. She was only sorry he did not sail as Gwyn did, for sailing was such an enthusiasm of hers and it gave her such a feeling of being alone and inaccessible that she would have found it doubly enjoyable with him.

Her own work suffered to some extent, although she had done nothing for some time before Van arrived, so he could not be held entirely responsible for her idleness, no matter what Gwyn and her uncle hinted. Her uncle, she thought, eyed her constant escort with less enthusiasm than she would have liked, but he said nothing and Sheena was determined to let nothing deter her from spending as much time as she could with Van.

They swam and walked and Sheena had the satisfaction of seeing the good-looking face, once so disappointingly pale, turn a stunning golden brown that showed up his blue eyes and blond hair even more flatteringly. She refused to admit that it also made him look a lot more like Gwyn, although the similarity was undoubtedly emphasized by the tan.

It was nearly two weeks after the picnic at Barbell Sands that Sheena saw Cora Lindsey again, and that in rather odd circumstances.

She had decided to walk after dinner, alone, since Van was always working in the evenings, and she almost instinctively headed for Lea Point, enjoying the cool breeze that blew in off the sea and the blessed calm of the evening.

She had much to occupy her mind and she thought mainly of Van, inevitably, thinking how much things had changed since he came to Lea Bay and how much more exciting her life had been in his company. The fact that he appeared to find just as much pleasure in her company gave her an added glow and not even Gwyn's persistent teasing could prise from her the knowledge that she was, almost inevitably, falling in love with Van. She hoped too that she had not misread the many small signs she thought she detected that told her he was getting more fond of her too, and she lifted her face to the cooling breeze, her eyes as dark as coals and shining softly.

She walked in a dream as far as the road back to the house and she had only just begun to notice that the hydrangeas were in full glorious bloom along the sea road when she saw Cora Lindsey. It was only a brief glimpse, it was true, but she was certain she recognized the neat brown head of the woman sitting in the front passenger seat of a car parked on the road by the kerb.

To make quite certain she looked again as she passed a gap between two of the shrubs and confirmed her own identification; not only that, but there was also a man in the driving seat, and Sheena was pretty sure that a second before she turned her head the two of them had exchanged a kiss.

Whether Cora saw her or not she did not attempt to find out, for she did not look back again, keeping her head resolutely turned away, half wishing she had not seen the car or its occupants, especially in such intimate circumstances.

Gwyn, she remembered, had described Cora Lindsey as the siren of the secretarial pool and a very desirable property. Obviously the opinion was his own and just as obviously he enjoyed her company and found her attractive. How much more serious it was than that she had no idea, but it seemed someone else also found her a very desirable property and she wondered what he would have to say about that.

She would never have seriously considered telling him what she had seen, because she shrank from being deliberately hurtful, but she was puzzled and it gave her something else to think about beside her own involvement with Van. If Gwyn was more than interested in Cora Lindsey it was not her place to carry tales about her, but it could not stop her wondering what devious game the other girl was playing.

By an odd coincidence it was Gwyn himself who mentioned Cora the following day when he and Sheena were drying off after a swim, with the beach to themselves, as usual and the water cooling as the evening drew in. Their former easy companionship restored, she automatically handed him her towel and just as unconsciously he took it from her and dried the water from her back as he had always done.

'Are you sailing tomorrow?' Sheena asked as he handed back her towel, and he nodded, a slight grin touching his mouth as if something amused him, making her wary.

'I am.'

She had been rather hoping he would say no, for she had already arranged to see Van and the Sunday before she had had to decline her usual role as crew for the same reason. Much as she liked being with Van she disliked having to turn down the opportunity to sail with Gwyn, for they made an excellent team and had won quite a few prizes in the past as well as getting a great deal of enjoyment from it.

'I'm sorry, Gwyn.' She paused in her efforts and looked at him apologetically. 'I won't be able to crew for you.'

Gwyn laughed, a hint of malice in his eyes as he looked at her. 'I don't remember asking you to,' he told her. 'Not to worry, Tuppence, there *are* other people who sail, you know.'

For a second she regarded him curiously and not a little reproachfully, one hand holding back the fall of long hair that threatened to obscure her view, but his expression told her nothing. 'I'm sorry,' was all she said, and turned her head away, only to swing back quickly when his fingers curled round her arm.

'How sorry?' he asked quietly, studying her face as if he was trying to discover what she was thinking. 'Sorry you can't crew for me, sorry you're otherwise engaged – or sorry I am?'

He was only teasing, she knew, but there was an underlying hint of seriousness in his questions that she found discomfiting and she lowered her gaze after a second or two, vainly trying to shake off his hold on her arm.

'It doesn't matter, does it?' she asked. 'I – I just thought perhaps you wanted me to crew for you, that's all.'

'Ah, but what I want has nothing to do with anything when Cousin Van has priority, has it?' He laughed softly, shaking his head as if in sympathy. 'Poor old Tuppence, you've really got it badly, haven't you?'

She pulled her arm free at last and bent to retrieve the tunic she wore to cover her swim-suit, a warm pink flush colouring her face which she sought to conceal by swinging the thick curtain of her hair between them. 'I don't know what you're talking about,' she told him. 'As usual you're not making much sense.'

He reached out a hand and swept back the concealing hair, a smile on his face when he saw the betraying colour. 'No?' he said. 'Don't be bashful, darling, you're seldom apart from Van these days, except evenings as now, and I don't kid myself you'd be swimming with me now if Van wasn't working. If he was available I'd get short shrift, I've no doubt.'

'You didn't *have* to come!' she declared, sounding more indignant because she knew only too well that what he said was the truth.

'Would you rather I hadn't?'

The question was not only unexpected but sounded suspiciously like a challenge, and she looked a bit startled as she studied him for a moment before answering, 'No. No, of course not.'

'But you *would* rather be with Van?'

His insistence worried her for some reason and she shook her head slowly, silent for a moment or two while she pulled on the tunic and fastened it. He still stood watching her, glistening wet and uncannily still as if he laid much store by her answer.

'You'll get cold if you don't dry off,' she told him, seeking a change of subject to something she found less hard to answer.

She should have known he wouldn't be side-tracked and he shook his head stubbornly, still holding the towel in his hand unused. 'Don't try to change the subject,

Tuppence. I asked you a question and I don't think it's unreasonable of me to expect an answer. *Would* you rather be with Van?'

She did not answer for a moment, then shrugged her shoulders, reluctant to be honest, though, she told herself, he knew the answer well enough and it could hardly be that important to him. He was just being awkward, trying to embarrass her. 'All right,' she agreed at last, 'I – I suppose I would. Now are you satisfied?'

'Should I be?' His brown face crinkled into the familiar grin and he ran careless fingers through his thick hair where it curled damply over his ears, knowing she would not answer him.

She sat on her knees in the sand, watching him towel the worst of the water from his body, then shrug into the towelling robe he always wore to the beach. It was a familiar routine, but she had found herself lately noticing things that she had always taken for granted until now, and sometimes when she stopped to think, as now, it not only puzzled but worried her.

The way he ran his fingers through his wet hair and the way it always flopped over one eye when it was wet. He had a grace of movement too that was almost unbelievable in so big a man and she had only recently noticed it. Then there were those small, fine lines at the corners of his eyes and round his mouth, where he smiled so often. None of these things could have suddenly happened, but she had never before been so conscious of them and the knowledge made her uneasy. Perhaps, she told herself, her feeling for Van also made her more conscious of other men.

It was strange and not altogether comforting to think of someone else sailing with him in the sleek, polished intimacy of the *Sea Bird* too. The two of them had sailed together so often in *Sea Bird* since Gwyn bought her five years ago and she almost resented the idea of someone else taking her place, although in the circumstances she knew she was being unreasonable.

'Who – who's crewing for you tomorrow, Gwyn?' she asked as they walked up the beach to the road.

'Why?' A quizzical brow cocked the question at her bluntly and she frowned.

'I just wondered, that's all. If you have the right to question me for no reason at all, I don't see why I can't do the same to you.'

'Tit for tat,' he jibed, and Sheena glared at him.

'All right, *be* mysterious!'

'I'm not being mysterious, Miss Uppity. If you must know, it's Cora.'

'Cora?' She had expected almost any other name but that, and she blinked at him uncertainly for a moment.

A smile questioned her surprise. 'Why not?'

'Oh – no reason. I just wondered, that's all. I didn't know she knew anything about sailing.'

'She doesn't know a lot,' he admitted, 'but if I could teach you I can teach Cora. She's a pretty smart gal and I can't see her hanging herself with the sheets.'

It was a deliberate and, Sheena felt, an unfair jibe at her own first attempt at sailing. She had been only fifteen at the time and very anxious to please. The fact that she had become entangled in the rope while endeavouring to extend their sail area to pick up more of the available wind was an incident he had always teased her about unmercifully. He had disallowed the fact that she was so young and that his old boat had been much harder to handle than *Sea Bird*.

'You'll never let me forget that, will you?' she asked reproachfully. 'I wasn't very old then and you were bullying me. I couldn't help being clumsy.'

Surprisingly he seemed to regret his teasing and one

55

arm hugged her close for a moment, his face against her hair as they walked. 'I know, Tuppence, I know. You've proved a damned good little sailor since then too, and I shall miss you.'

'Miss me?' She looked up hastily, hating the note of finality in the words, and surprised a look in his eyes that made her feel suddenly sad as if she had lost something precious.

'Well, I shan't be seeing much of you this summer, shall I?' he asked. 'With Van taking up all your week-ends I shan't get a look in.'

'Oh, Gwyn, don't!'

She would feel such a fool if she cried, she thought, but she really felt as if she might. It was as if all those happy years she had spent sailing and swimming with Gwyn were coming to an end and, much as she looked forward to a different sort of summer with Van, she hated to think the old days were ending. There was so much she would miss, that she already missed, for she had not been sailing since Van's arrival nearly three weeks before.

'It's not my doing,' Gwyn told her. 'You've been so busy with Van and it's likely to go on like that from what I can see, but I don't see why I shouldn't still go sailing. Cora volunteered to crew for me, I didn't have to shanghai her into it.'

She was silent for a moment. 'You've known her a long time,' she said.

'About twelve years.'

'As long as you've known me.' For some reason that idea was not easily acceptable.

'That's right,' he agreed with a glance at her thoughtful face. 'But Cora was already earning her living in the hard cold world and you were just a little shrimp then.'

Sheena by-passed the allusion to her eleven-year-old image and raised her eyes. 'That sounds like a dig at me,' she suggested, 'but it's hardly my fault if I've never *had* to face the – the hard cold world, is it?'

'Not at all,' he agreed. 'I was just passing comment on the differences, that's all. Nothing derogatory to either.'

Sheena shook her head, still thoughtful. 'Is she married?' she asked.

Surprisingly, he hesitated, seemingly caught unawares by the bluntness of the question. 'Does it matter?' he countered after a moment. 'She's a nice girl.'

So nice, Sheena thought bitterly, that she could offer to go sailing with Gwyn and still pass an intimate moment with some other man in a car only a short walk away from where he lived. If she did anything to hurt Gwyn she would – but then it was no concern of hers. Van was her interest, not Gwyn.

Sunday was very warm, but uncomfortably so, sultry rather than pleasant, and Sheena eyed the sky with some doubt as she prepared for her outing with Van. It would be much wiser to take a raincoat, no doubt, but she disliked the effect that had on her morale and chose to gamble on it changing for the better as the day wore on.

Van's car would be shelter enough for the two of them if it did rain, and the thought of being with him in the closed intimacy of the car gave rise to prospects she did not even dare think about.

Her uncle eyed her sleeveless dress and sandals doubtfully when she came downstairs. 'Aren't you taking rather a chance, Sheena?' he asked. 'It smells very much like rain and you know how it can whip up a storm in no time.'

'I thought of that,' Sheena confessed with a smile, 'but if it does rain we can always shelter in the car.'

'You're seeing Van Goalan again?'

Sheena frowned over the faint hint of disapproval she thought she detected, and nodded. 'Yes, we're going to Barbell Sands again.'

'Sweetheart – please don't think I'm trying to interfere.' John Cameron's good-looking face wore an unaccustomed worried look and he was obviously reluctant to voice his worry, though Sheena could guess only too well what it concerned. 'I hate acting like an uncle-cum-guardian,' he went on, 'but have you thought what you're getting into? It's very isolated at Barbell Sands and, while I'm not suggesting you'd do anything stupid, darling, Van Goalan does belong to a profession that – well, that treats things rather less seriously than most of us do.'

Sheena felt the colour in her face and knew there was an angry sparkle in her eyes, but she held her temper in check, mostly because she had never argued with her uncle in anger before and she would hate to do so now. Especially when Van was involved, because it made it look as if he was responsible in some remote way, and that she wanted less than anything.

'Uncle John, please don't treat me like a child.' She managed a smile that she thought successfully hid her feelings. 'Actors are no more promiscuous than anyone else, and you know it. Also you never raised any objections to my going to Barbell with Gwyn, so why should you mind if I go with his cousin? It's no more isolated now than it's been the past twelve years, you know.'

'I know.' He made the admission readily enough, but he was obviously still not happy about her going. 'Oh well,' he smiled wryly, eyeing her as if he only now realized she was no longer a little girl, 'I suppose I have to get used to the idea of you being a woman and not a child. My reluctance,' he added ruefully, 'stems from my having to admit that if you're older then so am I.'

'Oh, Uncle John!' She kissed his chin lightly, her resentment forgotten. 'You're still the handsomest man I know and you certainly don't have to worry about getting old yet.'

'It'll be when you get married that I shall really feel an old man,' he told her, and Sheena laughed, the colour coming into her cheeks when she met his speculative gaze.

'Don't worry,' she told him with apparent assurance, 'you'll be married before I am, I can forecast that with certainty.'

John's dark eyes, so like her own, surveyed her for a moment in silence and Sheena wondered if she had spoken too impulsively. 'You're determined to pin me down, aren't you, love? Did it never occur to you that Suna and I are quite happy as we are?'

Sheena, challenged on something she felt she knew something about, tilted her chin at him obstinately. '*You* may be,' she retorted, 'but Suna isn't.'

Her certainty seemed to startle him and for a moment he said nothing, only gazed at her with a slight frown between his brows, then he smiled wryly. 'You sound very sure of that,' he said quietly.

'I am, Uncle John.'

'Hmm.' He regarded her steadily. 'I know you and Suna are as thick as thieves and God knows what women talk about when they're together, so I'll take your word for it.'

'I – I didn't mean to interfere,' Sheena insisted, 'honestly I didn't, but – well, I like Suna, I like her very much, and I'd hate to think of her giving you up in despair.'

'You think that's likely?' He sounded quite serious, and Sheena nodded.

'Any woman can be discouraged if she sees no prospect of ever being asked the one question that matters.'

He smiled again now and his eyes teased her. 'I'll take

the expert's word for it,' he told her.

'I'm serious, Uncle John.'

He put an arm round her shoulders and kissed her gently. 'I know you are, sweetheart, and, believe it or not, so am I.'

'About Suna?'

'About Suna. Does that make you happier?'

Sheena smiled. 'It does, much happier. I can think of no one I'd rather have in the family than Suna, although she's a bit young to relish being called my aunt.' She glanced hastily at her watch when a short, sharp note on a car horn broke the Sunday morning stillness outside. 'That's Van,' she said, 'I'd better run. 'Bye, Uncle John!'

She knew he saw her go with his former misgivings rekindled, but she could do nothing about that. Being with Van was important to her and no matter who objected or raised difficulties she could not give up seeing him. She had not yet considered what would happen when he went away again, when the summer season was over and he returned to his more usual hectic way of life in London and wherever his rather erratic profession took him. Only somewhere at the back of her mind was the thought that possibly she would go with him, be with him for the rest of their lives, but that was still a too distant dream to ever consider yet.

Van left his seat, as he always did, and saw her into the car, his eyes registering approval of her appearance. 'You look lovely, as always,' he told her, dropping a kiss with practised ease on the nape of her neck as she slid into the car. 'I can never decide whether I like you best with your hair up or down.'

Sheena touched careful hands to the high-piled coiffure she had spent so much time on. 'I thought I'd have it up today for a change,' she said, feeling the rapid, disturbing thud of her heart against her ribs already. 'I'm glad you approve.'

He slammed the car door closed after himself and started the engine, his eyes making a swift, expressive survey of her face and hair. 'I always approve,' he told her.

They drove for a while in silence, then a heavy dark cloud rolled into view and frowned at them threateningly, while Van eyed it through the windscreen with a grimace of dismay. 'I have a nasty feeling we're going to get a downpour,' he forecast, 'in which case we shall have our picnic spoiled.'

'I thought it might rain,' Sheena remarked. 'It would, of course.'

'Of course,' he echoed, pulling a face. 'Never mind, we can always eat in the car, I suppose, although there isn't much room.'

'We'll manage.' She was looking across at the open sea, choppy and with the occasional white horses whipped up by the rising wind and racing towards oblivion with almost unbelievable speed, her thoughts rather surprisingly elsewhere. 'Gwyn's in for a rough time if a storm breaks out there,' she murmured, almost to herself.

It was evident that mention of his cousin did not exactly please him and a slight frown creased his brow for a second.

'He's used to sailing in rough weather, isn't he?' he asked.

'With an experienced crew helping,' Sheena agreed. 'Cora's only a learner.'

'Cora?' He turned his head briefly in surprise. 'I didn't imagine her as a sailor, so – that's the way the land lies, is it?' His meaning was obvious and Sheena found herself frowning over it.

'We usually do a lot of sailing,' she explained, 'and normally – I mean other years I crew for Gwyn, but since –

61

since I've been seeing you at week-ends and not able to go, Cora volunteered.'

'Good for Cora!' She thought she detected sarcasm, but would not have dreamed of objecting, although if it had been Gwyn in his place she would have done without hesitation.

Sheena looked at the choppy sea again and the darkening threat of the clouds and was rather surprised to find herself worrying. 'I can only hope Gwyn has the sense not to go out,' she said. '*Sea Bird* can be very temperamental in a variable wind and it looks as if it's blowing in all directions at once.'

He heaved a sigh, purely theatrical in its depth. 'Darling Sheena, Gwyn's a grown man and quite able to manage without you for one short trip at least, so do stop acting like a mother hen, there's a good girl.'

Sheena looked at him, startled to see the stubbornness on his face and a glint of hardness in his eyes even though, a moment later, he laughed and flicked her a teasing look. 'I'm sorry,' she apologized, feeling rather small. 'I suppose I was fussing a bit, wasn't I?'

'Too much,' he agreed, 'but I forgive you, my darling, if you promise to forget all about Gwyn and his Cora and give all your attention to me.'

'I promise,' Sheena vowed, but nevertheless felt a niggling twinge of dislike for that 'Gwyn and his Cora'.

The weather did not disappoint them after all and well before lunch time the wind dropped and the scudding dark clouds gave way to smaller white ones that drifted along lazily above the magic that was Barbell.

They swam awhile, then lazed on the beach until they felt like eating, and Sheena thought she had never been happier. Van was such a perfect companion, attentive and never too selfish about what they should do, although Sheena would not have dreamed of disagreeing with his suggestions the way she did with Gwyn. The expression in his eyes alone sent the blood pounding through her body like a glow of fire, giving a shine to her dark eyes and a flush to her cheeks. It was a wonderful world, she thought, as she packed up the remains of their picnic lunch.

'Shall we walk along the sands a little way?' he suggested as he stowed the depleted basket into the car, and Sheena nodded. It was all so wonderful that she was prepared to go anywhere he wanted to go. 'I don't mind what we do,' she told him with a smile that confirmed it, and he took her hand, drawing her closer to his side as they set off along the open, endless sands.

The dunes with their fringe of waving grasses ran the whole length of the way, shielding the common land behind them, the grasses blowing and turning with the ever-changing wind. There was the same feeling of timelessness about the whole stretch of coast for about two miles, Sheena knew from experience, and then the road veered seawards again and brought with it the disturbance of humanity and its attendant requirements.

'This place really does have a profound effect on me,' Van declared, smiling down at her.

'And me,' Sheena agreed. 'I feel as if, no matter how long I walk, I shall never come to the end of all this quiet and solitude, but of course I should.'

'Have you ever painted this part of the world?' he asked. 'This stretch of beach in particular?'

Sheena shook her head. 'No, I never have. I felt somehow that – that I could never quite capture the – the feeling of it. You know what I mean? It's very simple basically, just the sand and the sea and that fluttering grass on the dunes, but that's only what the eye sees, there's so much more to it than that. An – an atmosphere that I feel would elude me completely if I tried to put it

63

on to canvas.'

He nodded as if he understood, but was evidently set on getting her to try. 'Just the same I'd like you to try,' he told her. 'I'd like you to make that painting you promised me, one of this beach. Will you try? Just for me?'

It was a plea difficult for anyone to resist and Sheena found it impossible, so she nodded, albeit a bit uncertainly. 'I'll try,' she said, 'if you really want it.'

'I do.' He drew her even closer, putting an arm round her shoulders, setting her pulse racing anew when he rested his face briefly against her hair. 'I'd like always to remember this place, this summer, and this girl.' He spoke softly and kissed her brow where the thick dark hair began. 'Sheena.' This time his mouth sought hers and held her breathless for a long moment. 'Sheena,' he whispered against her cheek, softly. 'I want to remember you always.'

Sheena opened her eyes and looked at the hazy endlessness of the scene and smiled. 'I might be able to capture the – the magic of this place if I try,' she said, her voice almost breaking with the emotion that stirred in her.

'You can,' he assured her, 'because it *is* so special. You'll do it for *me*, Sheena, for me to take away with me and treasure always.'

She thought the sentiment charming and smiled over it, but she was reluctant to think of the time when this idyllic summer must inevitably end and she tried to dismiss the thought from her mind, smiling up at him determinedly bright. 'There's plenty of time for painting yet,' she declared. 'It won't take too long and – and you won't be going yet. You've only just arrived.'

'Not yet,' he agreed, 'but I always find the summer season goes so quickly.' And that, Sheena thought, was what she feared most.

CHAPTER FOUR

It was almost two weeks later, and very late on the Saturday night, that a knock on her bedroom door woke Sheena from her sleep. She lay for a moment, unsure whether she had actually heard anything or if she had been dreaming. There was a crack of light showing beneath her door and she thought she could sense someone standing out there, but before she could dismiss the whole thing as fancy another soft knock brought her out of bed and, sleepy-eyed, to the door.

She blinked for a moment in surprise to see her uncle standing there, his dark eyes smiling when he saw her sleepy face. 'Uncle John! What on earth's happened?'

She noted, vaguely, that there seemed to be an air of excitement about him that was unusual and a sparkling glint in the dark eyes that regarded her, almost impatiently, she thought. 'Sheena, please come downstairs for a minute, will you, darling,' he asked, 'just for a little minute?'

'But—' She glanced down at her nightdress and her bare feet. 'I can't come down like this, and it's nearly one o'clock in the morning. Uncle John, what's happened?'

Her mind was still too sleepy to guess the reason for his air of excitement yet, and she wanted nothing so much as to go back to her disturbed sleep. 'Darling, I'm sorry if you were asleep, but you more often aren't at this hour on a Saturday.' He glanced at his watch and smiled apologetically. 'Sunday morning,' he amended. 'Get a robe and make yourself respectable and come down,' he said persuasively, as wide awake as if it was midday. 'Suna's downstairs.'

'I see.' The reason for the excitement clear at last, she picked up her robe and put it on, not bothering to put anything on her bare feet. She followed him down the stairs still trying to skim the sleep from her brain, her hair, she realized too late, still tumbled and tossed from sleep.

He had said Suna was there, and she would not have minded too much appearing like that in front of her, but he had neglected to say there was also someone else, and Sheena stared in dismay when she saw Gwyn there too with Cora Lindsey.

'It's a celebration,' her uncle told her, apparently unconscious of his *faux pas* as he poured her champagne and handed it to her. 'We couldn't leave you out, sweetheart.'

Trying hard to ignore Gwyn's gaze which she thought both pitied and teased her, she raised her glass, smiling at Suna Blane in genuine affection. 'I can guess the reason,' she said softly, 'and nothing gives me greater pleasure than to wish you both every happiness. Suna, Uncle John, every happiness always.' She hugged Suna and her uncle and smiled delightedly at the picture they made, with Suna holding on to John's hand, looking as flushed and pleased as any young girl.

'Thank you, darling.' Suna glanced up at John briefly with a smile. 'I told John it was a shame to wake you when you were having an early night for once, but he would insist on you joining in the celebration and I'm glad he did; it wouldn't have been right without you.'

'Especially since you gave me the final push that made me take the plunge,' John Cameron laughed. 'Thank you, Sheena.'

'Oh, you'd have got there sooner or later,' Sheena told him, and Suna laughed softly, her grey eyes glowing as she looked up at her newly acquired fiancé.

'I feel as excited as a schoolgirl,' she confessed, 'which is most undignified at my age, but I can't help it.'

'It's not undignified at all,' Sheena denied stoutly. 'Not at any age, it's perfectly natural.'

'John wanted to celebrate,' Suna went on, 'and then we saw Gwyn and – and Miss Lindsey, and we just *had* to tell them our news.' She giggled happily into her champagne. 'So we decided to bring some champagne home with us and let you join in the party.'

'It was very sweet of you,' Sheena said, smiling, made aware again of the visitors, 'and I *do* wish you both every happiness for ever and ever.'

'Amen.' It was Gwyn's voice that added the pious hope and Sheena glanced at him, trying not to notice that the blue dress Cora wore, though quite simple, suited her perfectly and made her look very much younger. Trying not to notice too, the way Gwyn stood close to her, almost as if they were as much a pair as Suna and John.

'I didn't expect strangers in our midst,' she said, putting a hand to her tumbled hair, 'or I'd have done something about my appearance before I came down.'

'Oh, please don't worry on my account,' Cora begged, quite genuine in her assurance, Sheena felt certain. 'I only wish I could look half as good, hauled downstairs in the early hours.' It was maddening, Sheena decided a little unreasonably, that Cora Lindsey was so difficult to dislike. She really was, as Gwyn said, a very nice girl.

'It *was* a celebration,' her uncle emphasized.

'And even the kiddies are allowed up for celebrations,' Gwyn added, not quite *sotto voce*, and plenty loud enough for Sheena to hear and flush with resentment.

'Seven years don't allow you to be so – so superior,' she told him, not caring that anyone else heard and horribly conscious of her tumbled hair and bare feet.

Not altogether surprisingly, Cora sided with her,

looking at Gwyn reproachfully and in such an intimate way that Sheena felt a sudden and inexplicable loneliness in her. 'Sheena's right,' Cora told him, 'you shouldn't be so condescending. Those seven years may have counted for a lot ten years ago, but not now.'

'All right, all right!' He held up his hands defensively while John and Suna, picking up the gist of the argument, joined in Cora's laughter. 'They're ganging up on me, John,' he pleaded. 'Top up my glass and help boost my Dutch courage, will you?'

'Who's next in the matrimonial stakes?' John asked, brimming his glass for him, his eyes on Sheena. 'You told me I'd be married before you, Sheena, didn't you?'

'I was sure you would be,' Sheena declared, hoping to avoid a repetition of his original question which somehow made her uneasy. 'I was right, you see.'

'I've taken the first step,' her uncle agreed cautiously, 'but you've plenty of time to catch me up *and* overtake me, sweetheart. You young folks work fast.'

'Oh, Methuselah!' Gwyn taunted. 'You and Suna will be galloping up the aisle long before the rest of us have time to draw breath, isn't that right, Sheena?'

'I – I don't know,' Sheena demurred, suddenly and embarrassingly self-conscious at being questioned so abruptly. 'I can only speak for myself.'

The blue eyes sought and held hers determinedly, and his voice was quiet and soft as if meant for her ears alone. 'And what do you say?' he asked. 'Speaking for yourself?'

'I – I don't know, please—' She left the rest of the sentence unsaid, conscious of the curiosity in four pairs of eyes. Even her uncle was speculating and she felt horribly and helplessly vulnerable.

It was Suna who rescued her, perhaps unconsciously, when she glanced at her watch and smiled up at John.

'It's time I was going, darling. I know I shan't sleep, I'm much too excited, but it's well after one o'clock and I *do* have to see some wretched man about some business tomorrow.'

'I'll run you home,' John told her, and winked an eye at Sheena wickedly, 'but don't expect me *too* soon, will you, Sheena?'

Sheena shook her head, smiling to see him so obviously happy. 'I won't,' she promised.

Now that she was awake, Sheena knew she would have difficulty going back to sleep, so she saw the four of them out of the door, then went back into the sitting-room and picked up the empty glasses and the bottles, carrying them through to the kitchen.

There was a little wine left in one of the bottles and she poured it out, holding the glass up to the light, her expression thoughtful, perched on a kitchen stool with her heels hooked on to the bar. It was good news that her uncle and Suna had at last settled their future and she had no doubt at all that they would be very happy together, but it did raise the question of her own future and that, at the moment, appeared to be anything but settled.

She could scarcely stay on with her uncle after he and Suna were married, and that alone would be quite a wrench after spending fifteen years of her life there and loving every minute of it. Perhaps with Van – she shook her head, trying not to foresee how that would work out. It was cowardly of her, she supposed, but she hated to think of even her and Van anywhere else but here at Lea Bay, and that was simply not practical. He, at least, was required to move about the country, even all over the world, and she could not just stay here and expect him to come back to her each time, but the alternative was something she could not face at the moment.

She sighed and raised the almost flat champagne to her lips, grimacing at its lack of life. There were so many things to think about, and always, at the back of her mind, was the thought of Gwyn standing so near to Cora Lindsey and the close, intimate way she had reproached him for teasing Sheena.

She finished the wine, despite its flatness, and sat staring at the empty glass, wondering why something she had wanted so much to happen, now that it had happened, made her feel so low and gloomy.

Another sigh and she got off her perch and rinsed her glass, placing it carefully with the others in the rack to drain. She glanced briefly at the wall clock and saw that it was gone half past one; time she went back to bed and tried to get some sleep.

She was only half-way across the hall when she heard a car stop on the drive outside and smiled to herself. Evidently her uncle had taken less time to say his good nights than his rather facetious remark had implied, and she walked across to open the door for him.

It took her a second or two to realize that it was not her uncle standing under the porch light, but Gwyn, a bright devil of mischief in his eyes when he saw her. 'I saw the lights were still on,' he explained, 'so I took a chance on somebody still being up. May I come in?' he added when she did no more than stare at him rather vaguely.

'I – I suppose so.' She stepped back to let him in, more than ever conscious of her attire than she had been with all of them there. She glanced down at her bare feet and tried, vainly, to draw them out of sight beneath the robe, knowing he was aware of her move and finding it amusing. She was also uncharacteristically nervous with only herself and Mrs. Goodenough in the house, probably fast asleep in her little room at the back of the house.

'I left my cigarette case.' The way his eyes glittered at

her she knew he followed her train of thought and that he found that amusing too.

'Couldn't you have waited till morning?' she asked, trying to inject a note of practicality into a rather bizarre situation.

He was already striding with easy familiarity into the sitting-room where the light still burned and he tossed a short laugh over one shoulder as she followed him in. 'I could have,' he agreed, 'but *some*one was obviously still around, so I thought I might as well collect it now. You don't mind, do you?'

'Not in the least.' She hugged the flimsy robe to her and hoped he would find his wretched case quickly and go, but when he straightened up from the settee with the case in his hand, he showed no sign of being in a hurry to go.

The rugged brown face looked more tanned than ever under the yellow overhead light and his eyes had a darker blue look that she found disturbingly unfamiliar. It could be that the champagne he had taken on top of other drinks during the evening had some effect on him, but it was as if he was a stranger to her suddenly, and one she was horribly uncertain of.

He was looking at her in such a way that she felt the colour flood to her cheeks and her heart begin to pound relentlessly against her ribs, both sensations strange to her in the company of Gwyn, and it worried her.

'Aren't you pleased about John and Suna?' he asked, and even his voice sounded different, deeper and slightly husky in a way that did crazy things to her pulse, and she suddenly realized that it was probably her own unaccustomed imbibing of champagne that was making her feel so strange. It was almost as if both of them were entirely different people, both of whom she felt uncertain of.

'Of – of course I'm pleased,' she said, discovering her

71

own voice lower in pitch and trembling, which was utterly ridiculous.

He crossed the room to stand in front of her, his eyes still having that unusual dark blue in their depths, and they studied her face for what seemed like an eternity, then one finger lifted her chin gently. 'You've realized the repercussions it will have on you, haven't you?'

It was a guess so discomfitingly accurate that she did not want to answer. 'I – I hadn't thought of it like that,' she told him, untruthfully. 'I'm very pleased about Uncle John. I know he and Suna will be very happy and I – I'm glad for them.'

'But you'll be Little Orphan Annie,' he insisted, and she found him too discomfitingly close, his eyes on her mouth as if it fascinated him.

'I'm glad,' she insisted, trying to escape his hold, but he simply changed from holding her chin with one finger to cupping it in his hand and smiled at her frustration.

'Then why the long face?' he asked softly. 'You don't look very pleased about anything, Tuppence.'

'I *am* pleased, I *am*!' She wished he would go away and leave her alone, that she had the strength of will to turn her head away and not have him so close.

'Then smile, damn you!' The expletive was mild and he widened his own slightly crooked mouth into a grin. 'Come on, sweetheart, smile.'

The endearment was usually exclusive to her uncle and normally she would have objected to Gwyn using it, only this big, brown-faced man was not the Gwyn she knew, but a rather alarming stranger. An oddly exciting stranger, she had to admit, as she closed her eyes instinctively when his mouth covered hers, gently at first. It couldn't be Gwyn kissing her like this, it *must* be a stranger, but if it was— She opened her eyes suddenly and pushed against the arms that held her so tightly she could not even move an inch.

'Let me go!'

He looked startled for a moment, she thought, her own eyes wide with something akin to panic as she stared up at him, then the face was suddenly familiar again when he laughed, his arms easing their hold, but still enclosing her as he looked down at her flushed face and the tumble of dark hair, now more dishevelled than before.

'If you insist.' The return to normality seemed, for some inexplicable reason, to make her more self-conscious than ever and she wished she could simply run away, but it was impossible while he still held her.

'Please, Gwyn!' She pushed at his arms again and, to her relief, he slid them from round her waist, but slowly as if he might at any moment change his mind.

'You look like a little gypsy,' he told her with a grin, and she started back nervously when he grabbed a handful of her hair and tugged gently. 'Just like a raggle-taggle gypsy.'

'Well, what do you expect?' she retorted, trying hard to sound only normally indignant, and he laughed.

'Great expectations,' he declared solemnly, 'are often followed by great disappointments, so I've learned not to expect too much. Not at first anyway.'

He was deliberately enigmatic, she knew, and she shook her head to rid herself of the last of that dizzy feeling that had come so close to betraying her. 'Will you please go home?' she said, slowly, for she still felt uncertain of herself. 'I'm tired and I'd like to go back to bed.'

'I thought you'd have been there before now,' he remarked, pushing the cigarette case into a pocket. 'Did you finish the bubbly?'

She looked startled for a moment, then smiled admittance. 'What there was,' she confessed. 'I shouldn't have done, it goes to my head.'

One brow arched quizzically and he grinned. 'So I gathered from the shine in your eyes,' he told her, and she turned her head away hastily.

She would have closed the door on him without further exchange, but he turned before he went down the one step to the drive, and that dark blue gleam was in his eyes again. 'Good night, Tuppence.' He bent his head swiftly and kissed her mouth. 'Sweet dreams.'

Although neither of them mentioned the incident during the week that followed, Sheena felt that she was a little more wary of being with Gwyn than she had ever been and it made her sorry, more sorry than she could say. Not that it made any real change in their relationship, for they had been swimming three evenings out of six and there was still an air of easy camaraderie between them that had always existed.

She saw Van almost every morning that week-end, as the weather still held, they had continued their usual round of swimming and driving, only occasionally going for short walks because it was not Van's favourite form of exercise.

'It's good for you,' Sheena teased him one day when he objected.

'I get all the exercise I need,' he retorted. 'It's hard work being on stage for almost the entire show, you know.'

They were sitting on the end of Lea Point watching the sea licking at the sand and the endless ruffle of white-edged waves as they rippled all along the shore. 'Do you enjoy it?' she asked, without quite knowing why.

'Enjoy it?' The blue eyes looked round at her curiously as if the question should have been unnecessary, and he lifted his shoulders in one of the rather attractively continental gestures he often used. 'What else is there? It's my whole life, Sheena, I'm nothing without it.'

'I don't agree with that,' Sheena denied with a smile. 'You'd still be something special, even without the trappings of your stage personality.'

For a moment he studied her in silence, a half-smile on his face. 'You say that, but I doubt very much if you would even notice me without the trappings of my profession,' he told her, and sounded quite sincere about it. Without a sign of false modesty. 'There are plenty of good-looking men about, and you would probably do no more than register the fact in your pretty head and then forget about it ten minutes later.' He shook his head, smiling ruefully at her. 'No, darling, it's a sad fact but true, it's the glamour of my reputation you find so attractive, not me especially. You see, I have no illusions about it.'

It was so much as Gwyn had worded it that for a moment she was at a loss to know how to answer, then she shook her head again in the inevitable denial. 'Gwyn tried to tell me that when you first came,' she said, having no qualms about betraying Gwyn's opinion, 'and I disagreed with him too, because I think you're both wrong.'

He raised one of her hands to his lips and kissed its palm. 'It's so ungallant to argue with a beautiful woman,' he told her, 'so I shall accept your charming flattery and be thankful.'

Sheena knew the colour in her cheeks betrayed the way her pulse was hammering away at her temple, and it was inevitable that he knew it too, for he still held her hand, a small, secret smile on his lips. 'Have you any special preference for where we go tomorrow?' she asked, trying to steady her voice and keeping her eyes fixed on the rippling tide just below them. 'It scarcely seems possible the week's gone so quickly and it's – Sunday again tomorrow.'

She had taken his company for granted, used to seeing him each Sunday since he had arrived, and she had never even considered that tomorrow would be any different, so that for a moment she was stunned by his shaking head.

'I'm so sorry, darling, I should have told you before, but somehow it slipped my mind until you mentioned it. I can't see you tomorrow, I'm afraid. There's something I have to do, some tiresome papers to sign and publicity pictures to take – I don't know, my agent has arranged it and I have to be there. I really *am* sorry.'

'Oh, please don't be.' She felt embarrassed to think that she had taken him so for granted, almost as she did Gwyn, and that was something she would never be able to do with Van.

'But I *am*,' he insisted, and she believed him, partly because of the expression in his eyes and because she wanted to. 'I love being with you, Sheena, and I'd much rather stay here with you than be in town, please believe me.'

Sheena laughed softly, hoping she hid her disappointment successfully. 'My vanity insists I believe you,' she told him, 'even though you are being polite.'

The fingers holding hers tightened as he looked down at her, his eyes hinting at exasperation as Gwyn's sometimes did when she was being stubborn about something. 'I am not being polite,' he declared, 'and don't be so perverse, my darling, or I shall have to prove you wrong.'

She raised her eyes to him, some uncontrollable imp of provocation in them. 'I don't believe you,' she said softly, and shook back the long, dark hair that framed her face.

His arms went round her slowly, drawing her to him, so close she could almost feel the glowing warmth deep down in his eyes before he pushed her relentlessly down and down into the shifting warmth of the sand, and she closed her eyes as his mouth sought hers.

It was not the first time he had kissed her, but it was the first *real* kiss, and it was a moment she had anticipated with so much pleasure that she was surprised and a little disappointed to discover that her reaction was less deeply satisfying than she expected.

There was warmth and excitement in his kiss, but none of the gentleness she had expected, and something deep inside her stirred in protest, making her move uneasily after a second or two and put her hands against his chest as if to push him away.

'Sheena!' The whispered name was half protest and she opened her eyes and looked at him, almost as surprised as he was at her own reaction. There was a frown between his brows, and to add to her discomfiture, he reminded her too much of Gwyn now that his face was almost as darkly tanned as his cousin's.

'Van, I—'

'Don't pretend you didn't want me to kiss you,' he interrupted, his face still close enough for her to notice the different, harder look in his eyes.

'I'm – I'm not pretending,' she admitted. 'It's just that—'

Again he took up the challenge, though this time less aggressively. 'You didn't expect me to comply,' he guessed, completely wrong in his assumption. 'Well, I'm sorry, darling, but if a beautiful woman invites me to kiss her, as you did, I do my best to be obliging about it.'

He looked at her steadily for a moment and she wondered if her instinctive objection had ended their almost idyllic association, then he laughed softly and brushed his lips lightly against hers. 'Little girl!' he teased, and Sheena was reminded yet again of Gwyn.

She looked up at him, her eyes shining darkly, her heart racing the way it always did when Van was near her, and she hastily dismissed the small, niggling doubt that had made her protest. 'I'm *not* a little girl,' she insisted, and saw the deep glow in his eyes again as he brought his face closer.

'No,' he agreed softly, 'you're not.'

CHAPTER FIVE

SHEENA found herself almost regretting the fact that it was another bright and sunny day when she woke on the following morning, although she realized that her regret was merely a selfish gesture inspired by her disappointment at not seeing Van. If the weather had been wet and miserable, she told herself, she would not have minded quite so much that she was not seeing him for the first time in six weeks.

She sighed, thinking how quickly she had grown used to being with him. How quickly she had learned to like being with the man rather than the exciting and not quite real star she had first been impressed with. The time had flown unbelievably fast and already the summer season was more than half-way through. The few remaining weeks would no doubt go just as quickly and before she knew where she was the end of the season would be upon them and Van would be leaving along with all the other people who brought the world of glamour and excitement that went to make up an English seaside summer. Only now Van had become too important to her to face losing him.

She lay there for a while, wondering what it was that was important enough to take him away from her for the whole day. Things to sign, he had told her, pictures to be taken, so she supposed it concerned his future plans. Other theatres where he would appear, other towns, other crowds of adoring fans surrounding him in a nucleus of worship and excitement. It was a life he admitted he enjoyed and had no desire to change, and what worried her most was that she found it so difficult to picture a place for herself in the hectic, ever-changing chaos of it all. Somehow she would have to learn to adapt, but it would not be easy.

Her uncle noted her rather doleful expression when she joined him for breakfast and, guessing the reason, half-smiled to himself. 'I imagine you're at a loose end with Van Goalan away,' he remarked. 'Would you like to come with Suna and me to Portlea? Nothing very exciting, just a run along to the cove and lunch at the Dragon.'

Sheena smiled but shook her head. 'No, thank you, Uncle John. It's very sweet of you to offer, but I'm quite sure neither you nor Suna want company. I'll be quite happy here on my own, don't worry.'

He did not deny her assumption that he and Suna would prefer their own company, but raised querying brows over the rest of her answer. 'Haven't you managed to inveigle Gwyn into taking over?' he asked, a smile taking any suggestion of spite out of the question.

Sheena frowned, shaking her head. 'I haven't *tried* to inveigle him, as you call it,' she told him. 'And anyway, I've been given my marching orders as Gwyn's crew, so he wouldn't want to know.'

It was an inaccuracy that her uncle did not overlook and he arched doubtful brows as he spoke. 'I rather thought it was the other way round,' he remarked. 'That you've been too occupied elsewhere lately to bother. *You* gave Gwyn his orders, didn't you?'

It was the truth, Sheena recognized, but put so bluntly it made her look selfish and unthinking, and she disliked the idea of that. 'I only missed one Sunday sailing with him and he decided I wasn't coming any more,' she protested. 'He took Cora Lindsey as his crew without even asking if I'd be free to go with him.'

'Would you have been free to go with him?'

She eyed him for a moment, a niggly suspicion at the

back of her mind that he had been discussing her with Gwyn, and the idea did not please her at all. It was probably Gwyn's fault, she told herself, that her uncle did not take to Van more readily. 'I – I didn't know,' she admitted grudgingly. 'How would I know from one week to the next?'

'Well, you couldn't expect him to do without his sailing whenever you were occupied with Van Goalan, could you?' he asked reasonably, and Sheena admitted it with a shrug.

'I don't know. Van *has* asked me to go out with him each Sunday since Gwyn's had Cora crewing for him, but he knew I was *free* to go with him, so it didn't matter.' A dark brow lifted expressively and showed his opinion of that excuse and Sheena bit her lip. 'Anyway,' she added, 'he probably prefers to have Cora aboard. She knows less about it and he can bully her more easily than he does me, especially as he's her boss in a manner of speaking.'

Her uncle decided to ignore the implication of that. 'They make rather an attractive pair, don't you think?' he asked, and Sheena looked at him suspiciously. 'I thought so when they were here the other night.'

Reminded of her own thoughts on that subject at the time, Sheena frowned. 'I – I don't know that I'd thought of it like that,' she said, 'but I suppose they do.'

'She's a very nice girl,' John added, unconsciously or conciously adding fuel to the flames.

'So Gwyn said.' She tried not to sound sarcastic, but doubted she succeeded.

'And he's known her a long time too.'

'He told me that too. He's known her twelve years, as long as he's known me – us.' She hastily amended the personal implication, then looked at him curiously, something just coming to mind that had not occurred to her before. 'Surely you must know her as well,' she said, and managed to make it sound like an accusation. 'She works for you.'

'She works in the secretarial pool,' he corrected her quietly, 'and they are not a section of the company I come into contact with very often, though I've seen her possibly half a dozen times, to notice her anyway. Gwyn met her when he was working his way through the business, I believe.'

'So he said.' She remembered again that brief glimpse she had caught of Cora Lindsey and the man in the parked car along by Lea Point. 'Has she a boy-friend?' she asked.

Her uncle looked at her curiously. 'I don't know the private life of every pretty girl in my firm,' he told her, 'much as I'd like to, but she's a very attractive woman and I don't imagine she's any more nun-like than the rest of her sex.' He cocked a curious brow at her. 'Why?'

Sheena shrugged. 'Oh, nothing really, I just wondered if there was anyone else besides – besides Gwyn.' She sipped her coffee thoughtfully, wondering what Gwyn's reaction really would be if he knew about the other man. Unless of course he already knew and accepted it.

Once breakfast was finished, Sheena had to admit to far more of a sense of loss than she would have thought possible. It could have been, of course, that she had never before been quite without company, and the thought of not having Gwyn to fall back on seemed the worst part of all. Ever since she had known him, Gwyn had always been there when she wanted him. Boy-friends had come and gone, particularly in her teens when she had cried away the end of many a seemingly endless passion on Gwyn's broad shoulder. Once she had found her niche and decided to take her undoubted artistic talents seriously, she had spent more time in Lea Bay and therefore opportunities had been less than in the social hurly-burly of Sandlea, but there had still been the occasional flirtations with romance and the same shoulder was still there when things went wrong.

After breakfast she did assorted little jobs that had been neglected for too long while she was otherwise occupied, but they were done all too soon and she wandered downstairs again rather aimlessly, wondering what she could do to occupy her time. She could, she supposed, start painting again, but somehow she did not feel like it. Inspiration was definitely at a low ebb today.

Instead she went out into the garden and stretched herself full length in a cane chair with a footrest, finding the sun had a soporific effect before she had been there very long. So drowsy did she become that she did not hear a sound of anyone approaching until she opened her eyes to find Gwyn standing at the foot of the chair with a wry grin on his face.

'I thought it was only old ladies who fell asleep in chairs,' he told her.

Sheena looked up at him through half-closed eyes, uncertain, now that he was here, whether she was glad to see him or not. 'Why aren't you out sailing?' she asked without preamble and without stirring from her reclining position.

Gwyn laughed, pulling a wry face at her form of greeting. 'Good morning, Gwyn,' he told himself cheerfully, 'how are you?'

'I can see how you are,' Sheena remarked dryly. 'But I can't see why you're here and not out in *Sea Bird*.'

'Because I waited for you to crew for me,' he declared, 'and since you haven't volunteered, I've come to conscript you.'

She still made no effort to move, but looked at him steadily from under her lashes, suspicion rearing its ugly head, that he had only asked her because for some reason

Cora Lindsey was not available. 'Why?' she asked bluntly.

'Why not?' he countered, and sat himself on the foot-rest of her chair, elbows on his knees, laughter in his eyes as if he recognized her suspicion.

'I thought you'd given me the sack,' she said, 'that's why not, and anyway, I'm nice and comfortable here and I'm not sure I want to move.'

He slapped the limp arm nearest to him and grinned. 'You lazy little tyke,' he told her. 'Come on, do you want to crew for me or not?'

Sheena stirred lazily without sitting up, trying to look as if the last thing she wanted to do was to exchange her comfortable chair for the more energetic duties on board *Sea Bird*. 'I don't know,' she demurred. 'I'm a bit out of practice.'

'Nonsense!' He dismissed that excuse derisively with an impatient hand.

'Where's your usual crew?' she asked. 'Isn't she available?'

His grin showed that he followed her reasoning all too easily and he looked over his shoulder at her steadily. 'If you mean Cora,' he told her, 'she isn't coming over today.'

Sheena closed her eyes again, as if she had every intention of going off to sleep. 'Bad luck,' she told him.

'So-o—' He drawled out the word, his head nodding understanding. 'We're playing hard to get, are we?'

'Not at all,' Sheena denied airily, 'I'm just not sure *I'm* available either.'

'Oh, you contrary little cuss!' he laughed. 'Either you get out of that chair right now and come with me volun-tarily or so help me, I'll sling you over my shoulder and press you into service.'

'Captain Bligh!' she retorted, opening her eyes and smiling despite herself.

84

He smiled down at her, sensing her weakening and playing on it as he always did. 'Come on, Tuppence,' he coaxed, 'it's time you came out with me again, you'll be getting rusty.'

'You rather scornfully said nonsense to that when I suggested it,' she reminded him, and he gave a snort of exasperation and reached for her hands, hauling her upright in the chair. She sat for a moment looking at him, her eyes betraying her willingness but still determined to be stubborn about it. 'I'm not sure I *want* to come,' she told him, 'especially as I'm only standing in for your girlfriend.'

'I thought that was it,' he declared, laughing at the slight pout that softened her mouth into fullness. 'You never did like playing second fiddle, did you, Tuppence?'

Sheena eyed him resentfully for a second, wishing he did not always so accurately interpret her motives. 'I don't see why I should,' she said. 'You're only asking me to come because your – your Cora is otherwise engaged, and I don't relish being told, first, that I'm no longer wanted to crew for you because *she's* doing it from now on, and then rounded up like a – an absconding deckhand when she can't come.'

'*I* didn't take the job from you,' Gwyn declared, 'you did that yourself by spending every Sunday with Van. You didn't expect me to stay on dry land because you were gallivanting with Cousin Van, did you? Have a heart, darling, I don't see why I should hang about all summer because you've got a bad cardiac case for my glamorous cousin.'

'Oh, you're just—' She stopped herself in time making the accusation, but she thought he guessed at it from the sly, knowledgeable smile on his face. She looked down at her long slim legs, golden brown below the brevity of shorts. 'Anyway, it's no thanks to you that Van *has* gone on taking me out, considering you did your best to spoil it that first Sunday he was with me by having all those—' Again she bit her lip on the rest of the accusation, unwilling to voice the suspicion that had been at the back of her mind ever since that first Sunday at Barbell Sands.

'Go on,' he said, too quietly for Sheena's peace of mind, and she shook her head. 'I'd like to hear what charming little ideas you have running around in your head, so let's hear it, Tuppence. What did I do?'

'Oh, forget it!' She did not want to go into it, she decided too late, for he would not let it drop now, she knew that well enough.

'I don't want to forget it, not yet anyway,' he told her insistently. 'I want to hear what you suspect me of.'

'You're dramatizing,' she accused, 'I'm not suspecting you of anything.'

'You little liar, you are, and I think I know what it is, but you're going to tell me. Come on, spit it out!'

'Oh, all right!' She looked down at her fingers, twisting them together endlessly until he clamped one of his big hands over them and held them still. 'First of all you came along on our picnic,' she told him, '*and* brought Cora. You can't have forgotten that.'

'Oh, I haven't forgotten,' he said, a glint of laughter in his eyes for her reluctance, 'but I'm still trying to work out who you resented most, both of us – or just Cora.'

She looked at him for a moment without speaking, then looked down at her fingers again, still firmly held in his grasp. 'I didn't want anyone there but me – me and Van.'

'O.K., so I'll believe that for now. Now – what else am I supposed to have been guilty of?'

'You know quite well what else,' she retorted.

He turned himself right round to face her as near

straight as his rather precarious perch allowed and put his hands to her arms, shaking her lightly, the amusement in his eyes temporarily giving way to exasperation. 'You *tell* me,' he ordered, 'and make it convincing.'

'Oh, stop *bullying* me!' She tried in vain to free her arms, but he held her firm, his expression as relentless as his grip. When he did not speak she shook her head, more uncertain than ever now. 'You know quite well,' she told him. 'All those people from that – that coach party. You told them where they could find Van, it would be easy enough to drop a word in the right place and you know so many people. You were angry because I forgot about sailing with you.'

'And you think I went to all the trouble to tell someone about Van's plans with you so that a party of holiday-makers could hunt him down, just because you let me down over a sailing date?'

Put like that, Sheena thought, it sounded horribly conceited on her part and also very unlikely on Gwyn's. He really would not go to all that trouble just to pay her back for breaking their date, and her eyes when she looked at him acknowledged it at last. 'You see how potty the whole idea is?' he asked quietly, a smile seeking to console her now that she had seen sense, and she nodded.

'I – I can see it now,' she admitted. 'But who – I mean someone must have—'

He shook his head at her, smiling wryly. 'Hadn't you thought of our Mrs. Groome?' he asked, and Sheena frowned, genuinely puzzled. 'Her sister's the cleaner at the Bay Coaches offices,' he told her, 'and she chattered about Van to her, knowing she's a fan just as our Mrs. Groome is. She was better informed in the first instance than I was, you see,' he added wryly. 'She knew you and Van were going to Barbell Sands a day or two beforehand and, gossip being what it is, it got round to some enterprising member of the staff at Bay Coaches, then—' he spread his hands in a fair copy of Van's continental-style shrug, 'Bob's your uncle.'

'I see.'

He studied her half defiant, half regretful face for a moment with a smile. 'Am I still the villain?'

Sheena looked up, determined not to give in too easily, although she had been embarrassingly wrong about him, she recognized, and she should apologize. 'I'm – I'm sorry about the coach party,' she said at last, 'but you *did* invade our picnic, and you *did* bring Cora Lindsey.'

'And I *am* interested to know which you're most angry about,' he countered softly, his eyes agleam with devilment. 'The fact I gatecrashed your party or the fact that I brought Cora?'

It was a question Sheena was not prepared to answer and she bit her lip as she swung her feet to the ground, leaving him in sole possession of the chair. She would have walked off into the house, but before she could move out of reach he took one of her hands and held it while he got to his own feet, looking down at her in a curiously gentle way that made her feel suddenly rather sad, though heaven knew why.

'Will you come sailing with me, Tuppence?'

The appeal, made in his most persuasive voice, had the inevitable effect and Sheena nodded, curling her fingers round the hand that held hers, completely forgetting that she had intended making some telling remark about Cora's other man-friend.

'Shall I change?' she asked, and responded to the broad grin he gave.

'Not for me,' he told her. 'I'm not averse to the combination of long legs and short shorts.'

There was only just enough wind to make sailing worthwhile, but to Sheena just being on the water again was pleasure enough after all the weeks of abstinence. She felt a glow of delight as the little craft tacked busily chasing a lazy, elusive, off-shore breeze, and just being out here on the quiet water with Gwyn gave her a feeling of reassuring normality.

Once or twice she caught his eyes on her and smiled instinctively, only once wondering if this same state of trusting intimacy existed between him and Cora when he came sailing with her. She found the prospect not to her liking and dismissed it determinedly.

It was only as they walked along the beach afterwards, on their way home, that she mentioned Cora, and then with a reluctance that was overcome only by sheer curiosity. Gwyn held her hand as he usually did when they walked on the sand and he glanced down at her quizzically when she raised the subject of Cora.

'Why didn't – couldn't Cora come with you today?' she asked.

'You were right the first time,' he told her.

She considered for a moment. 'Didn't?' she guessed, and he nodded. 'You don't know why?'

'No.'

'Oh, I see.'

He smiled at her wryly. 'I doubt if you do, Tuppence,' he told her. 'In the first instance I know Cora had something else to do today, though I wasn't inquisitive enough to ask what, and in the second place, I hadn't intended asking her today, but she didn't know that.'

'You hadn't?' He shook his head. 'Oh, oh, I see.' She was not sure she did see, but she had some vague idea why he had not invited Cora Lindsey over that particular Sunday and the feeling of pleasure it gave her was a surprise in itself.

'Oh, I see.' He mocked her expression and her tone. 'Do you really see, or are you just making one of your wild guesses?' he asked. There was amusement but also a look of gentleness on the rugged brown face as he looked down at her, the inevitable fall of hair half covering his brow, which he combed back with his fingers.

'I'm not saying anything else,' she said warily, afraid of saying the wrong thing. 'I might – I might be accused of sounding too sure of myself again if I do.'

To her surprise he laughed. 'That's never bothered you before,' he told her. 'Don't tell me modesty is a newly acquired virtue, darling.'

Her mouth pouted reproach and she looked up at the laughter in his eyes. 'I didn't know you considered me as – as conceited as all that.'

'Not conceited,' he declared, 'just self-assured, Tuppence, like most beautiful women.'

'If you consider me a beautiful woman,' she retorted, not to be outdone, 'you could surely find a more suitable name for me than Tuppence.'

He laughed again, shaking his head over her reaction. 'Then maybe I should call you by my paternal grandmother's name,' he suggested, 'though I doubt if you'd like it any better, you're such a contrary little monkey.'

Sheena was intrigued in spite of the jibe. 'Tell me,' she urged. 'How can I tell if I like it or not otherwise?'

'Anwen.' A raised brow anticipated her reaction.

'Is it Welsh?'

'As the hills,' he replied with a smile, 'and it means very beautiful.'

Sheena wrinkled her nose in doubt. 'It's a very nice meaning,' she demurred, 'but I'm not sure I like it very much. I wouldn't like to be *called* Anwen, even if it does mean very beautiful. I'm sorry, I know it was your grandmother's name, but it doesn't really *sound* like very beautiful somehow, does it?'

'I told you you were a contrary little monkey,' Gwyn

chuckled. 'My grannie was something of an authority on Welsh names and their meanings and she would have found an appropriate one for you, I don't doubt – probably the same one she had for my Aunt Blodwen.'

Sheena looked at him suspiciously. 'What was that?'

'Cadwen.' He looked down at her, his eyes glittering devilment. 'Yes, I think I'll call you Cadwen instead of Tuppence, as you don't like it.'

Sheena frowned over it. 'What does Cadwen mean?'

He chuckled again, shaking his head. 'I don't think I'll tell you,' he teased, 'not today. You've had enough flattery for one day.'

'Tell me,' Sheena demanded, now throughly suspicious of him. 'Don't be so mean, Gwyn!'

'I'm not being mean,' he denied with a grin. 'It won't hurt you to puzzle for a while.'

She looked up at him her eyes curious. 'I suppose,' she murmured darkly, 'that Gwyn means nasty and unkind.'

He laughed and shook his head, evidently finding her hint amusing. 'You're quite wrong,' he told her. 'My grandmother chose it for me. According to her it means fair, which I am.

'Incidentally,' he added with a wicked gleam, 'half the meaning of Cadwen is fair, too, though not in the sense I've used it.'

'Oh, you're just trying to confuse me!' Sheena accused crossly, and continued walking in an air of dignified silence, although she still held his hand.

Sheena was not really surprised when Gwyn came for her after lunch, sounding the familiar strident summons on the car horn. She had lunched alone and was anticipating the afternoon rather dolefully with the company of a book which she dropped in her haste to get up. She waved from the window and Gwyn signalled her to come out and join him.

'Where are we going?' she asked, pushing the window wide, and he grinned.

'Does it matter?'

For a brief moment, she considered, then she shook her head. 'No,' she agreed. 'Give me a minute, Gwyn, and I'll be with you.'

'You have exactly five minutes,' he informed her with the old familiar arrogance. 'After that you're on your own.'

Her response was perhaps more childish than ladylike, but he laughed gleefully at the tongue she poked out at him and the way she wrinkled her nose as she banged the window shut with a smile.

It was less than five minutes until she joined him and he grimaced approvingly at her speed as he saw her into the car. 'Where *are* we going?' she asked, and he grinned at the inevitable curiosity.

'I thought you wouldn't be content with a mystery trip,' he told her. 'How does Sandlea suit you? Not too proletarian for you, I hope?'

'No, of course not. I used to go there a lot when I was younger, you know that.' She was nevertheless puzzled by his choice of destination, for he was usually no more fond of crowds than she was herself, but she was content, at the moment, to let it pass without comment.

'But you're intrigued,' he guessed, and laughed when her expression told him he was right.

'Not exactly intrigued,' she denied, 'just puzzled. You're not much more fond of Sandlea than I am as a rule.'

'True,' he allowed, 'but I feel like doing something different, something slightly crazy and not at all suited to a business man at all, so bear with me, will you?'

Sheena laughed. 'Certainly, we'll go anywhere you like,

but I can't agree that you *ever* behave like the conventional business man. Not my idea of one, anyway,' she added when he pulled a face at her. She was silent for a moment as they drove along the coast road. 'You've no special reason?' she asked.

'No special reason,' he echoed, and added with a laugh, 'you're a suspicious little devil, aren't you?'

'No, I'm not,' she denied, but smiling. 'I just wondered, that's all.' She settled back in her seat, content to leave it all to him and just enjoy herself. 'It'll make a change.'

Sandlea was certainly a change from Lea Bay, for Sunday was little different from any other day here. The crowds in their bright holiday clothes thronged the promenade, a kaleidoscope that was ever-changing, noisy and good-natured. Hot dog stands, ice cream kiosks and souvenir shops jostled for the available space on the sea front and vied with each other for the custom of the passing crowd. It was certainly different and not altogether unexciting if one knew it was only for a few hours.

They drove along the promenade looking for a space to park, getting nearer all the time to the gigantic fun fair at the far end and its strident, compelling music could be heard from several hundred yards away, reminding Sheena of the days when she had regularly come here with her friends.

'When did you go to the fair last?' Gwyn asked, backing the car into what appeared to be the only parking space for miles.

Sheena smiled at the paper-hatted passers-by with their accompanying huge swirls of candy floss. 'Not since I came with Teddy Pearson when I was seventeen,' she admitted. 'We quarrelled bitterly and I thought the world would come to an end there and then.'

'I think I remember that one,' Gwyn told her with a grin. 'Wasn't he the short, puny infant with a spotty face and greasy hair? You really had the most appalling taste sometimes, Tuppence, it was pathetic!'

'Oh, you were always so horribly superior,' Sheena objected. 'You always acted as if you were so high and mighty and we were a lot of ill-mannered babies, and we weren't, you know, we were just normal healthy teenagers.' She flicked him a brief meaningful glance as he helped her from the car. 'I'm not sure *you've* changed,' she added. 'You still look down your nose at my boyfriends.'

'Do I?' He took her arm, smiling enigmatically as he guided her through the crowds on the promenade. 'Well, what do you say? Shall we take the plunge into this masochistic maze of pleasure or not?'

The blaring tangle of sounds and the peculiar oily, hot engine smell of the fun fair suddenly seemed almost as exciting as it had a few years ago, and Sheena nodded, a sparkle in her dark eyes that was answer enough.

They drew the line at comic hats, but indulged themselves at the candy-floss stall and joined other adventurous couples on the waltzer and the big wheel. They were drawing breath after the water chute and passing the Tunnel of Love and Gwyn cocked a querying brow at her.

'Shall we?'

Sheena, for some reason, felt unsure of taking the challenge. She had been through the tunnel often enough with boy-friends in the past and been as scared of the spooky surprises as was expected of her, but that had been when she was younger, and never with Gwyn.

'I – I don't know,' she demurred, listening to the echo of shrieks that issued from the darkness of the tunnel.

'Scared?' She looked at him dubiously. 'What of?' he taunted softly. 'Me or the tunnel?'

Sheena flushed to have her doubts so accurately interpreted. 'Certainly not of you,' she retorted, and glanced at the garish entrance to the tunnel again, lifting her chin defiantly. 'I just think it's – it's childish, that's all,' she decreed, and flushed when he laughed out loud, so that several people passing by turned and looked at him.

'Childish?' he said, still laughing. 'Oh, darling Tuppence, you have to be joking. Why, this whole thing's childish – that's the idea of it.'

'Well – well, I don't want to go in that silly tunnel,' she insisted, 'and you don't either. You just want to – to make me look silly.'

He sobered then, his eyes contrite as he looked down at her, holding her hand tightly in his while he sought to reassure her. 'I had nothing so unkind in mind,' he told her softly, bending to make sure she heard him, his face close to hers, looking, she realized, as if they were lovers making up a quarrel. 'Please believe me, Tuppence.'

She glanced up at the brown face, so familiar and understanding in this garish, alien world, and she smiled. 'I'm sorry,' she said. 'I *was* silly, but I didn't want to go in that – that place. You didn't mind too much, did you?'

The old familiar grin answered her and he still held her hand as tightly as before. 'Now am I supposed to be honest or say what you want me to say?' he asked, and she frowned curiously. 'Do I say I didn't want to go in,' he enlarged, 'or do I tell the truth and say I did – but I wish I'd been Van and then you wouldn't have had any qualms at all?'

Sheena did not answer for a moment, her mind racing with the realization that she had, until this moment, forgotten about Van. She could not let Gwyn know that, however, and she merely shook her head. 'Let's not talk about it any more,' she told him, 'since you seem set on being difficult.'

It was difficult to know exactly what was in his mind when a moment later, after a long searching look at her face, he raised her fingers to his lips and kissed them gently. 'I'm sorry, Tuppence,' he said softly.

The time passed unbelievably quickly and the myriad lights on the amusements were already beginning to outshine the daylight when Gwyn looked at his watch. They were standing by the counter of a brightly lit kiosk drinking coffee and eating large, tasty hamburgers and Gwyn grinned at her broadly over his cup.

'Have you any idea what time it is?' he asked.

'No idea at all,' Sheena declared, making no effort to check with her own watch.

'It's nearly a quarter to eight,' he informed her. 'We've been here over four hours.'

Sheena laughed, swallowing another mouthful of hamburger. 'It doesn't seem possible,' she said, 'but I suppose it must be, it's getting dusky already.' She looked up at the sky, looking darker than it normally would because of the brightness of the lights all round them. 'I suppose we'd better be getting back.'

There was a hint of wistfulness in her voice and Gwyn smiled at the picture she made. Her almost black hair was untidy and loose about her shoulders, her cheeks flushed and her eyes shining like coals in the yellow light of the kiosk. 'Have you had fun?' he asked, smiling as if he knew the answer well enough, and Sheena nodded agreement.

'I've enjoyed it enormously.' She popped the last of the hamburger into her mouth and cleaned her fingers on the paper in which it had been wrapped. 'I've had a wonderful time, Gwyn, thank you.'

'Better than with Teddy Pearson?' he asked, teasing her, and laughed at her moue of reproach.

'Much better,' she agreed, 'and *we* didn't quarrel.' As if

the remark reminded her of their brief disagreement about the Tunnel of Love earlier, she lowered her gaze and shook her head.

'No, we didn't,' he said softly, obviously following her thoughts. He disposed of the paper coffee cups and returned to her with a smile. 'Well, Miss Hastings, if you're ready, we'll start for home. Does Mrs. Goodenough know where you went, by the way?' he asked, and Sheena nodded. 'Oh, good, then John won't worry in case you've been kidnapped.'

'Oh, he won't worry if he knows I'm with you,' Sheena told him wryly. 'It's only when I'm gone any length of time with Van that he has forty fits.'

'Oh?' He sounded genuinely surprised. 'Do I gather he isn't in favour of Cousin Van?'

Sheena glanced at him, a bit suspiciously, wondering if he was being deliberately obtuse.

'I think you know as much about that as I do,' she said. 'I know he talks to you about – about me and Van.'

The fact that he did not immediately answer only confirmed her suspicions. 'We've both known you for a very long time,' he said at last, in quiet contrast to the cheerful banter he had been using. 'We – we do occasionally worry about you.'

'Because of Van?' He nodded, taking her hand again automatically as they walked along the promenade to where the car was parked. 'Well, I can't think why you should,' she told him. 'After all, he's your cousin and – and in some ways he's very like you, I can see it repeatedly.'

His laugh was perhaps less amused than ironic and he shook his head firmly. 'I can't,' he denied, 'and I can't see where you find any basis for comparison. He's good-looking, which I definitely am not, he has the glamour of his profession, and God knows there's little enough glamorous about an export and shipping company. He loves the bright lights and the crowds of adoring fans who, quite frankly, would make me run a mile rather than face them.'

'Oh, you've only picked on the bigger, more obvious points to compare,' Sheena complained. 'It's in the – the little things that he's like you, only sometimes, but—' She frowned, seeking for words to explain how many times she had been reminded of him when she had been with Van. 'Oh, I can't explain. It's just little things – certain gestures, the way he frowns, only tiny things, but things that remind me of you.'

'I'm not only surprised you even notice little things about me,' he told her softly, 'but that you have time to think about me when you're with Van.' There was an intimacy in the gaze he turned on her and sufficient implication in his words to bring the colour rushing swiftly to her cheeks, and she was glad of his preoccupation with the car keys that gave her the chance to recover without his noticing.

They had driven along the promenade and were passing through the more residential part of the town, away from the crowds and in the less garishly lit streets. It was still not quite dark, but the street lamps were on and made pools of shadow where they failed to reach the valleys between them.

'That's where Cora lives,' Gwyn informed her, pointing ahead to a tall white-fronted house on the right-hand side of the road.

Sheena looked across, interested in spite of herself, and was just about to ask if Cora occupied it all or only rented a room, when something familiar caught her eye and kept her silent for a moment.

There was no mistaking the low rakish shape of Van's white car, parked outside the house, nor the appropriate number plate that betrayed its owner. The fair handsome head was unmistakable too, but there was some doubt about the identity of the passenger he was helping so solicitously from the front seat. Some doubt, that is, until she straightened up under the yellow glare of the street lamp over her head, smiling gratefully at the man who assisted her.

'Cora Lindsey!'

She knew Gwyn must have recognized her too, but he said nothing for the moment, merely accelerated past the parked car as if he was afraid of being recognized himself, and for several miserably silent minutes neither of them spoke.

'I suppose you're busy jumping to conclusions?' Gwyn said at last, and flicked her an inquiring glance over his shoulder.

'I don't have to,' Sheena said bitterly. 'It's all too obvious, isn't it?'

'I don't know,' he demurred. 'Why not leave the recriminations until you know the facts, Tuppence? It's usually safer, you know.'

Forgetting how her last conclusions had led her into thinking that Gwyn had been responsible for the coach party episode, she plunged headlong into her own version of what she had seen. She thought angrily of Van's apparently genuine regret that he could not spend today with her as usual and how willingly she had believed him. Her own self-confidence, she supposed, was responsible: she had been so sure he would not go away unless he had to and now she knew the bitter truth. He had spent the time instead with Cora Lindsey. Perhaps they had been to London, as he had said he was doing, but he had obviously not been alone.

'Oh, Gwyn, for heaven's sake!' she exclaimed miserably. 'What other explanation could there be? He told me he was going up to town on – on some business to do with signing papers and having photographs taken, and he wasn't – he was with *her!*'

'And you were with me,' Gwyn pointed out quietly. 'No harm in changing partners for a day, is there, darling?'

Sheena did not answer, but sat determinedly angry and miserable all the way back to Lea Bay. It wasn't fair, she told herself, that her lovely day should have to end like this, and by the time Gwyn stopped the car in front of her uncle's house, she was feeling sorry enough for herself to cry when he looked at her.

'I'm – I'm sorry,' she told him miserably, 'but it was – was such a shock when I saw him there with – with her. After he – he told me—'

'Oh, Tuppence, come on now, there's no need to get so upset about it, surely.'

'There *is*,' Sheena insisted. 'You – you wouldn't understand.'

'Wouldn't I?' he asked, one eyebrow cocked at her wryly.

'I – I love him,' Sheena confessed wretchedly. 'I love him, Gwyn, and I thought he loved me.' She viewed his expression of doubt with a reproachful pout. 'I knew you wouldn't understand,' she told him. 'And you can't say I'm always falling in love with people, because I'm not.'

'I must admit,' Gwyn confessed, 'you've grown out of your penchant for undying passions lately. I supposed you'd grown up.'

'Of course I have,' Sheena declared. 'That's why this is – is different. I love him, Gwyn, I really do.'

To her surprise and chagrin, he was smiling to himself when she looked up at him. 'Darling Tuppence,' he said, putting an arm round her. 'I know how you feel, and I know you aren't just a little girl having a crush on some ghastly boy, but – well, darling, you do sound very like your seventeen-year-old self crying over young Teddy Pearson.'

The familiar and comforting broad shoulder was too convenient to ignore and she buried her face against it despite his jibe. 'Oh, you – you don't understand,' she sobbed, her voice muffled by his jacket. 'I'm not seventeen now and I love Van.' She still hid her face against him, his arm comfortingly reassuring round her shoulders.

'I know, darling, I know.' He held her as he had so many times before, his chin resting on her soft hair, and she was too immersed in her own misery to hear the words he murmured softly to himself, 'Here we go again!'

CHAPTER SIX

Even after a night's rather restless sleep Sheena was still undecided about what to do when she saw Van Goalan again. She was sorely tempted to carry on as usual and say nothing, but on second thoughts she mistrusted her own ability to do that. Somehow, sooner or later, she knew she would inevitably betray the fact that she had seen him with Cora Lindsey. It was possible that he would tell her himself, of course, and she rather hoped he would, because then she would know there was nothing to worry about.

Whether to say anything or not would have to wait until she saw him and knew how she felt. There would not be too long to wait, for almost certainly Van would be coming for her during the morning. Cora Lindsey was working during the day, so there was no chance that he would be with her today.

She bathed and dressed, still rather dreamy-eyed and indecisive, and when she went down to breakfast her uncle looked up, brows arched over her air of pre-occupation.

'Is something wrong, Sheena?' he asked as she poured herself coffee, and she shook her head.

'No, not really.'

He had been curious the night before when she had come in with a woebegone and tear-stained face, but he had said nothing then, merely looked surprised because he knew she had been with Gwyn. Gwyn often aroused her to anger, but he had never yet reduced her to tears and she could imagine that her uncle had been very curious, but still he had said nothing. Obviously this morning he intended being less reticent.

'I thought you were with Gwyn yesterday,' he said, and Sheena nodded.

'I was.' She had no intention of being too forthcoming unless he was very insistent, although she knew that only concern for her was behind his curiosity.

'Did you have a good time?'

'Mmm, very nice. We went to the fair.'

He looked a little startled at that, then half-smiled as he looked at her straight face. 'I see. Then maybe I should quote, Oh dear, what can the matter be, now that you've been to the fair?'

'We had a marvellous time at the fair, as I told you,' Sheena insisted, not altogether pleased that he was being so facetious.

'Oh, so I can take it that it wasn't Gwyn who made you cry?'

Sheena shook her head. 'No, of course not. Gwyn's never made—' She realized that her defence was probably a little too vehement when she saw her uncle's brow lift in comment. 'It wasn't Gwyn who made me cry,' she stated, more calmly. 'Anyway, I hadn't been crying very much, only a – a little weep, that's all.'

'Without appearing to be a nosey elderly relative,' John asked quietly, 'may I ask who *did* make you cry?'

'You're not a nosey relative of any age,' she told him, and could not resist answering the smile he gave her, but she was a little wary of telling him the reason she had been so upset last night. She could not forget that only a short time ago he had warned her that people like Van took some things a lot less seriously than most, and last night's incident would seem to prove him right at first glance, although she was still reluctant to admit it.

'I was just being silly, I suppose,' she admitted after a moment's thought. 'It's – it's just that when we were on our way home last night we – we passed the house where Cora Lindsey lives. Gwyn pointed it out to me.'

'And you saw her?' It was more statement than question.

'Yes.' She felt the same bitterness over again when she thought of what she had seen under the street lamp, and her mouth tightened for a moment.

'With Van Goalan.' This time it was definitely a statement and Sheena looked at him across the table suspiciously.

'How – how do you know?'

Her uncle smiled wryly. 'I wouldn't have dreamed of mentioning it normally,' he said, 'but when I was taking Suna home yesterday evening, we passed Van Goalan in that unmistakable car of his and I was pretty sure it was Cora Lindsey with him. Suna thought so too.'

'It was,' Sheena confirmed shortly.

'Did you know he was seeing her?' John asked, then supplied his own answer before she could speak. 'No, of course you didn't or you wouldn't be so put out about it now.'

'In the circumstances don't you think I have a right to be – be put out?' Sheena asked, and he looked at her quizzically.

'I can't answer that, sweetheart, unless I know the circumstances you refer to, can I?'

Sheena felt uneasy suddenly under his scrutiny. She had not hesitated to tell Gwyn, quite openly, that she was in love with Van, but somehow it was not so easy to say as much to her uncle. Although they had always been very close she had seldom if ever involved him in her emotional upsets. Not that she thought he would lack sympathy, but it had never been a thing she found easy to discuss with him.

'I – I'm very fond of Van,' she told him, stopping short

of the whole truth.

'Only fond of him?' The dark eyes that watched her had a gentle persuasive warmth that encouraged her.

'I – love him,' she said more certainly, and he nodded as if it was exactly what he expected to hear.

'I see. Well, in those circumstances, Sheena, don't you think you might be jumping to conclusions? I know you've spent a lot of time with Van Goalan since he's been here and Gwyn's spent a lot of time with Cora lately, at weekends, but surely if you can go out with Gwyn on the occasion that Van isn't available you can't really complain if Cora and Van get together, can you?'

Sheena was not prepared to let that go without objection. After all, Van had told her he had business in London, he had said nothing about taking Cora with him. If he had then her uncle's reasoning would be valid, as it was she could not see his argument.

'It's not the same at all,' she declared. 'The point is that Van told me he had business, some photograph session or something.'

'Cora's been crewing for Gwyn the past few weeks, hasn't she?' John said thoughtfully. 'Why wasn't she with him yesterday?'

Sheena frowned. 'She told Gwyn she couldn't go sailing with him, but she didn't say why. Being Gwyn,' she added, 'he didn't ask why, of course.'

'Wise man,' her uncle commented wryly.

'He wasn't going to ask her over anyway,' Sheena retorted, feeling more than ever the injured party since her uncle seemed as disinclined to condemn Van as Gwyn had been last night.

Her uncle raised a brow. 'Oh, wasn't he? Well, it looks like a straightforward case of change partners, doesn't it? And that's not such a bad thing once in a while, is it, sweetheart? After all, you had a good time with Gwyn.'

Sheena declined to answer that, so she finished her coffee and got up from the table and walked over to the window. Perhaps, she thought, she had exaggerated things rather. Maybe her feeling for Van made her see things a bit out of proportion, as Gwyn and her uncle suggested.

'Is Van coming for you this morning?' her uncle asked, and she shook her head uncertainly.

'I – I don't know. I don't know anything.'

'Poor old girl!' It could have been Gwyn offering his rather tolerant and amused sympathy, she thought, and turned reproachful eyes on him.

'I don't find it quite so easy to treat it as a joke, like you and Gwyn apparently do,' she told him. 'I don't think either of you realize how I feel, Uncle John.'

He left his seat at the table and joined her in the wide bay window, one arm settling comfortingly round her shoulders. 'I think we do, sweetheart, but there's nothing to be gained by looking on the black side, is there? After all, you haven't heard Van's side of it yet, have you, so you don't know what explanation there may be. Why not wait and see what he says, Sheena, before you go and upset yourself over it too much?'

'I should,' she admitted, looking at the dark eyes watching her sympathetically. 'That's what Gwyn advised me to do last night.'

Her uncle shrugged. 'There you are, I said he was a wise man, didn't I?'

Sheena smiled wryly. 'I'm sure he'd agree with you wholeheartedly,' she told him, and glanced at her watch. 'If Van *is* coming for me this morning he'll be here any time now and I'd better make myself more presentable, especially since I have competition.'

'Not really serious competition,' her uncle assured her,

obviously relieved to see her in better spirits. 'Of course,' he added thoughtfully, 'with a man like Van Goalan, sweetheart, every woman he speaks to is a potential challenge. If you *are* serious about him you'll have to face that fact along with a lot of others equally hard to take.'

'I know,' Sheena admitted. 'There's an awful lot I have to learn to accept and to adopt to – but I *will* learn, I must.'

It was about his usual time when Sheena heard the strident summons of Van's car horn from the front of the house and sighed her relief audibly as she went to answer it. She deliberately slowed down her pace so as not to appear too breathlessly anxious to see him, but smiled as she came out of the house.

Whatever she had meant to say as a greeting she was forestalled by his taking her in his arms and kissing her. 'Darling Sheena!'

She looked up at him wide-eyed and, she had to admit, a little wary, although her heart thudded impatiently at her ribs. 'Van—'

The blue eyes looked down at her, half apologetic she could have sworn, but she got no further than his name, for he held up a hand to silence her, pulling a rueful face. 'Please – don't tear into me, my darling,' he pleaded in mock fear. 'I can't take any more this mornng.'

Sheena looked genuinely puzzled. 'Van, I don't understand.'

'You were going to explode into righteous indignation, weren't you?' he asked, and Sheena loked at him, shaking her head slowly. 'Weren't you going to demand explanations, tell me what a two-timing no-good so-and-so I am? And that I'd better have a damned good answer or I'll get broken into little pieces?'

Sheena did not answer right away, too stunned by the

unexpectedness of it. Evidently he believed that attack was the best form of defence and he was disarming her before she could say anything at all. But if he knew all about her seeing him with Cora then either he had seen them go past in the car or Gwyn had already told him.

For a moment she absorbed the idea and the more she thought of it the more likely it sounded. Those words he had used, the threats, sounded exactly like quotations and she could almost hear Gwyn making them.

She looked at him uncertainly. 'I – I wasn't going quite that far,' she told him, 'but I had thought of asking you about—'

'Well, you don't have to,' he interrupted, pulling a wry face. 'I've already been given the full treatment by Gwyn, big guns and all. I know I was with Cora when you saw me last night and, believe me, I'm damned glad I have a clear conscience about it or I'm sure I shouldn't be here to tell the tale.'

Sheena blinked, scarcely able to grasp the full meaning of what he was saying. 'You mean Gwyn actually – he told you we'd seen you last night?'

'Did he not!' Van agreed fervently, looking as if he did not relish the memory of it. 'Darling, if ever anybody *does* treat you badly that cousin of mine will hang for him as surely as God made little apples.'

Her pulse, Sheena told herself, was racing so fast with sheer relief because he had as good as denied there was anything between him and Cora, but the idea of Gwyn becoming so aggressively angry on her behalf had, she was forced to admit, a certain fascination. It was simply not like Gwyn to lose his temper over anything. 'I – I didn't intend Gwyn should say anything about it,' she told him, almost apologetically.

Van arched an expressive brow at her. 'You didn't incite him to the attack with your big dark eyes?' he asked, looking as if he only half believed her.

'No, of course not! I didn't want him to say anything, let alone behave like – like that.'

Van kissed her after a second or two eyeing her thoughtfully, and helped her into the car. 'Well, heaven help us if you ever do,' he murmured fervently. 'Your champion does a very thorough job, darling.'

He drove them out on to the sea road while Sheena still tried to absorb the full meaning of Gwyn's unprecedented behaviour. He had often provided a willing shoulder for her to cry on, but he had never, in all the years she had known him, actually taken his intervention any further, until now. Apparently he had taken her seriously when she told him she was in love with Van, seriously enough to try and discover just why he had been with Cora Lindsey, which was something she did not yet know herself.

'Where are we going?' she asked, more to break the silence between them than any other reason.

Van glanced at her briefly and smiled. 'Your favourite place?' he suggested.

'It's yours too, isn't it?'

'Mine too,' he agreed.

They drove in silence for a while and Sheena began to wonder if he intended enlightening her about Cora Lindsey as he had done Gwyn. 'It's a lovely day,' she ventured at last. 'A good wind too.'

He cocked a half-amused eyebrow at her. 'What you mean is a good sailing day,' he suggested, and Sheena nodded.

'Like yesterday,' she said. 'We hadn't much wind yesterday, but it was lovely on the water.'

'Mmm, I can believe it. It wasn't so good in town, it was noisy, dirty and close, which only goes to show how much Lea Bay has spoiled me for town life.'

'Did – did you get your business affairs sorted out? You had some photographs to have done and some papers to sign, you said.' She did not look at him when she spoke, but lifted her face to the wind, warm but refreshing. It blew her long hair out behind her, cooling her cheeks and making her half close her eyes. She sensed rather than saw him turn his head briefly to look at her.

'You don't really care about the business side at all, do you, Sheena?' he asked, and she chanced a short, express-ive glance at him.

'If you mean am I curious about you – you being with Cora, yes, I am, but I wasn't going to ask about it because you seemed not to want to talk about it again.'

'I don't especially,' he admitted, 'but if you want to know about it I'll tell you.' He glanced at her again and pulled a wry face at the serious expression she wore. 'Goodness knows what crazy ideas are running around in your pretty head, although Gwyn gave me a pretty fair idea.'

'You don't *have* to tell me,' she told him hastily. 'You've been through enough with Gwyn, by the sound of it.'

'So I'll tell you exactly as I told him,' he insisted. 'It was pure chance that I saw Cora Lindsey at all. She was waiting at a Green Line bus stop just a little way out of town and I nearly didn't spot her because I was going so fast and it was already getting a bit dusky.'

Sheena's heart gave a skip at the sheer simplicity of it. 'So you stopped and gave her a lift back to Sandlea,' she guessed.

Van nodded. 'She'd been to see her mother, so she said,' he went on, 'and she'd left later than she intended or she wouldn't have been there at all. I couldn't very well leave the poor girl at the roadside, could I?'

'Of course you couldn't,' Sheena agreed readily, suddenly light-hearted, 'and I had no right to ask you about it or to make such a fuss.'

He looked at her again curiously, a faint smile touching his mouth. 'You thought I'd spent the day with her in town,' he said, his tone hinting at reproach.

'I – I didn't know what to think,' she confessed, appealing eyes turned to him. 'I'm sorry, Van.'

To her surprise he laughed softly, one hand leaving the steering wheel briefly to cover hers. 'Possessive as well as beautiful,' he declared. 'I should be flattered, shouldn't I, darling?'

Sheena was uncertain whether he liked her being so possessive or not; his voice had a hint of impatience, but that could have been her imagination playing tricks, and he certainly had that glow of warmth in his eyes when he smiled at her a second later. No matter if he did belong to his adoring public or if he took Cora home, there were still so many days to enjoy as they would enjoy this one, and she still had Van to herself most of the time. That must mean something.

They parked the car as usual and walked along the seemingly endless beach, just above where the tide lazily licked its way inland. Van's left arm was round her shoulders and they spoke hardly at all, both apparently occupied with their own thoughts. Sheena thought she could be happy with no more than this for a long time and she wished with all her heart that this day could go on for ever.

'Penny for them.' The blue eyes looked down at her, warm and smiling, and she felt the colour in her cheeks as she avoided his gaze.

'I couldn't possibly sell them,' she told him, 'not even for much more than a penny.'

'Dreams?' he guessed, and laughed softly, almost as if he guessed the gist of them.

'Dreams,' she agreed, 'and you shouldn't laugh, Van. They're very precious to us lesser mortals, you know.'

Her choice of phrase made him smile. 'Lesser mortals?' he echoed. 'Surely you don't class yourself as a lesser mortal, darling? You're among the goddesses.'

'Van, don't be sarcastic, please.' It was his tone as much as the words that prompted her to protest, but he pulled her close to him and kissed her gently.

'I'm not being sarcastic, my darling, I swear it. You're very beautiful. Why, every time I see you coming out of the sea I'm reminded of the birth of Venus and my poetic soul starts composing sonnets to you, like some latter-day Bill Shakespeare.'

His extravagance made her shake her head, but she felt a tingle of excitement too. 'I'd love to hear some of them,' she told him, her eyes teasing.

He looked down at her steadily for a moment, then hugged her again and buried his face in the soft, wind-tumbled hair. 'Like your dreams they're not for sale,' he told her. 'It's this place *and* you; the combination is irresistible, you both inspire me.'

'I'm inspired too,' she laughed softly. 'At long last I really think I might be able to start on that painting I promised to do for you, or have you forgotten all about it?'

'I certainly have not,' he averred. 'I've only been waiting for you to be in the right mood to start on it.'

'Well, I think I might be able to now,' Sheena said. 'I feel as if I might be able to capture some of the atmosphere of it.'

He bent his head and kissed her, his eyes glowing with such warmth that she felt her whole being respond to some inner urge that made her head spin. 'I knew you would,' he told her softly. 'Start tomorrow, darling, while you're still in the right frame of mind.'

'I'll try,' she promised.

He kissed her again, softly beside her mouth, then looked ahead of them to the glitter of sand and sea and the endless quiet solitude of it. 'Paint it exactly like this, darling, it has such – such life. It's primitive and exciting and surging with life.'

She looked up at the tanned, good-looking face with the rather long blond hair blown awry in the wind and saw an almost fanatical glint in the blue eyes. A tiny shiver that could have been fear trickled briefly along her spine, aroused by something she could not yet define, and she wondered if she could ever quite capture the feel of Barbell or the effect it had on both of them.

'Can't you see it?' Van asked, still in some dream of his own that she could only glimpse at. 'If you try, darling, you could imagine man in another age from this, walking where we're walking, even more aware of his surroundings than we are, though less conscious of it.'

'You love this place as much as I do,' Sheena said softly as the blue eyes looked down at her again, and he smiled.

'Love isn't quite the word I'd choose,' he told her. 'It's something stronger than that.'

'*Is* there anything stronger?' she asked, genuinely puzzled, and he laughed. It was a laugh that had an alien sound to it and somehow made her feel suddenly far apart from him as if she did not know him at all. 'Van.' She felt horribly unsure of him and rather more conscious of their isolation.

'Oh, don't look so wide-eyed and scared, darling,' he told her, a hint of amusement in his eyes. 'I won't go berserk and attack you.'

Sheena flushed. 'I never thought you would,' she protested.

He kissed her gently, his gaze still half-amused. 'Soon

everyone will be able to share this wonderful place, darling, the whole world will know about it and get the *feel* of it.'

Sheena was still suddenly, something warning her of what was to come. 'Van, I don't understand. What do you mean?'

He laughed again and hugged her tight, obviously very excited about something. 'I mean, my sweet, that I wanted to come here today, just once more, to see if it was a – a fluke or if there really was something about Barbell Sands that gets me.' He looked down at her, full of his excitement and thinking of nothing else. 'And it works, darling, it really does work.'

'What – what works?' She felt left out of things suddenly and rather unimportant. 'Van, what are you talking about?'

'Why, the magic of Barbell,' he teased her, too elated to notice the look in her eyes as realization dawned. 'The – the feeling it gives me each time we come here.'

'I know,' Sheena agreed, low-voiced, 'it works for me too, Van, but—'

He held her in his arms. 'Sheena, they're making a picture next year, an outdoor epic, and I've been given the lead.' He looked around him, his eyes glowing as he imagined the scene in another time, another situation. 'Darling, don't you see, I could act my heart out here, on this beach. Act as I've never acted before. The part fits me like a glove, and now—' he swept a hand round in a gesture that was purely theatrical, 'this place, it's all I need to make it an award-winning job, I know it is.' Sheena was silent, but it seemed not to matter to him, for he needed no encouragement as he visualized his triumph. 'I've already told my agent about it,' he went on, 'and they're going to get permission to use it.'

Sheena could not meet his eyes, so full of enthusiasm

and anticipation for his scheme, and she had not the heart to blame him, although the idea appalled her. 'You're going to use Barbell Sands to make a film?'

'We hope so. The wheels have already been set in motion and it's only a matter of time.'

'I see.' It could be more than a matter of time Sheena realized. There would be the local residents to contend with and they would not easily fall in with any scheme that was likely to spoil their locality. Not least of his antagonists would be Gwyn, and Sheena felt the dismaying inevitability of something much more personal when she felt herself obliged to side with Van simply because she could not bring herself to do anything else. The glow in the blue eyes and the way he kissed her made quite sure of that.

CHAPTER SEVEN

ALTHOUGH she hated to think of Barbell Sands overrun with film makers and all the paraphernalia of their profession, Sheena simply could not blame Van too much. He felt as strongly about Barbell as she did herself, but in a different way, and one of the facts she had to face was that anything to do with his work would always come first. If he could achieve something special by making the film at that particular spot then she had no right to deny it to him.

She could not bring herself to point out that its very isolation and quiet were the real magic of the place, or that the thought of its destruction hurt her deeply. Instead she told herself that if Van was prepared to share the spell it had for him with the whole world then she could hardly be less unselfish.

She had reckoned on Gwyn's reaction to the idea being fairly strong, but even so she was surprised, when he joined her on the beach that evening, to see him more angry than she had ever seen him. He said little when he joined her and that in itself would have been cause for comment if she had not realized the reason for it. There was a glitter in his blue eyes and a tight, close look about his wide mouth that even banished the laughter lines at its corners.

He swam out much further than usual and Sheena was hard put to it to keep up with him, eventually voicing her protest to the rapidly disappearing figure. 'Gwyn, wait!' She gave up finally and trod water, watching his fair head draw still further away from her with the glistening sweep of his powerful arms as they drew him through the calm sea.

It was almost ten minutes before he returned and she thought he seemed a little less tense and angry as he came alongside her in the water. 'I thought you'd have gone back,' he told her, with no hint of his usual banter, and Sheena shook her head slowly.

'I didn't try to keep up with you. I thought – I thought you seemed as if you wanted to go on for ever.'

There was a speculative look in his eyes as he looked at her for a moment without speaking. 'I did toy with the idea,' he said at last, and his smile was more expressive than humorous. He paddled lazily beside her for a moment and neither of them spoke, then he looked at her with more his usual expression and reached out a hand to touch her face lightly, almost as if the gesture were an apology. 'Race you back to the beach,' he challenged.

Even after the long and tiring swim he had already done he still strode out of the water ahead of her, reaching back with one hand to pull her alongside him. He smiled, as he always did, when she pulled off the confining cap and shook her hair down about her shoulders, and she breathed a sigh of relief for the sign of normality.

'Do you feel better?' she ventured, glancing at him from the corner of her eyes, and he looked up from his vigorous work with a towel to eye her speculatively.

'Better than what?' he asked.

'Oh – oh, nothing.' She realized now it had not been a very good idea to raise the matter of his earlier mood, but she saw from his expression that he had no intention of letting it pass.

'You asked did I feel better,' he said. 'You must have had some reason.'

'No, no, I didn't.'

'Sheena!'

Sheena sighed resignedly. 'Oh, all right! Well, of course I had a reason. I suppose you're not going to deny you were in a filthy temper when you came down, are you? You nearly bit my head off when I spoke to you.'

He grabbed a handful of her hair and tugged. 'Good job I didn't,' he retorted. 'It's what keeps you afloat, being hollow.'

'Don't *do* that!' She swung the long sweep of hair out of his reach, over one shoulder, and pulled on her tunic. 'After that display when you first came out here,' she went on, now bent on revenge, 'you have no room to call me bad-tempered.'

'Well, you are,' he averred, 'and I don't claim to be any more all sweetness and light than anybody else, far from it. I'm slow to rouse, but when I am roused – you watch out, my girl.'

'But I haven't done anything,' Sheena protested, and he laughed.

'No, it's not you this time,' he agreed, 'it's that – that moronic boy-friend of yours.'

Sheena flushed, not only about Van but to hear him referred that tone of voice. 'If you mean Van 'please don't refer to him like that.'

'Well, you seem to recognize him, from the description,' he retorted, flinging down the towel and shrugging into the same old towelling robe he always wore.

'He's *your* cousin,' she reminded him, 'he can't help inheriting some mutual characteristics.'

'I don't suppose he can,' he agreed, annoyingly amenable. He pulled her down to sit beside him. 'And there's a difference in the way we feel about him,' he added. '*I'm* not gooey-eyed about him.'

Sheena swung her dark hair back, her chin tilted at an angle of defiance, intent on bringing the cause of his ill-humour into the open now that he had angered her. 'I suppose Van's told you about his new film?' she guessed, prepared to defend his cousin at all costs.

'He told me about the proposed desecration,' he retorted, 'and he told me you agreed with it, something I find hard to believe.' The blue eyes looked at her steadily, trying to make her meet his gaze – something she felt unable to do at the moment. 'Do you?' he asked.

'Van loves Barbell as much as we – as I do,' she protested. 'He knows how I feel.'

'Does he? Did you really agree that his wretched film people should be allowed to swarm all over that beach?' Strong fingers lifted her chin, none too gently, and turned her to face him so that she was almost forced to raise her eyes. 'Did you?' he demanded.

She knocked his hand away and rubbed her face. 'I – I didn't say I agreed,' she admitted, 'but neither am I blaming Van for what he's done or proposing to do.'

'Oh no, you wouldn't!' He sat hugging his knees to him, the angry look back on his face and in his eyes again.

'How can I blame him?' Sheena asked, exasperated and despairing of ever making him understand. 'His – his work means so much to him, and if he feels that Barbell can help him with that, then he's entitled to do what he did.' She looked up at him, wide-eyed but not very hopeful. 'He says it may help him to get an award next year when the film comes out. He has a feeling for the part and for the place, it will be the greatest thing he's ever done.'

'Oh, lord, you sound like a blessed fan magazine,' he told her with a short laugh. 'Don't you mind that Barbell will be ruined?'

'Of course I mind.' She felt again the unhappiness it gave her to think of the peace and tranquillity of the sands destroyed for ever, as it inevitably would be, but she still refused to blame Van for being responsible. 'But – but I just can't blame Van, not altogether, Gwyn, I just can't.'

He looked at her, such a look as she had never seen on his expressive face before and which she instinctively shrank from. 'My God,' he said bitterly, 'you *are* crackers about him, aren't you?'

'I – I love him.' Somehow it seemed much more difficult to say it this morning than it had last night when he had been gentle and understanding. This Gwyn was a stranger to her, as much a stranger as the one who had come back to the house on the night of her uncle's engagement, only this one filled her with dismay and not excitement.

'You love him!' He echoed her words, but she had a feeling he did not believe them. 'So you don't say a word when he proposes destroying something we've always enjoyed, just to satisfy his professional ego.'

'I – I couldn't,' she confessed, a sudden urge to cry like a child misting her eyes when she looked at him.

He said nothing for several minutes while the tears began to roll, one by one, down her face. 'If you want a shoulder to cry on,' he told her bluntly, getting to his feet, 'you'd better call on Van, it's his privilege now.'

'Gwyn!' She stared after him as he strode up the sandy incline to the road, his long stride unhindered this time by her presence, and he did not even turn his head once to look back.

She watched him disappear, across the road and up the drive to the house, an awful cold feeling of finality in her heart that did nothing to diminish her tears. It was no use wishing for Van to be there to console her for, unlike Gwyn had been, he was not readily available, always there when she needed him – and that was just one more thing she had to get used to.

For quite a long time after Gwyn had gone she still sat there on the sand hugging her knees, her eyes dark and woebegone, looking and feeling desperately alone as she had never been before. It would not be easy without Gwyn, but if he intended behaving as he had tonight she would have to get used to it.

Whether Gwyn chose times when he knew she would not be there or whether he did not go swimming any more in the evenings, Sheena did not know, but she saw nothing of him at all during the rest of that week. She found swimming alone far less enjoyable than in his company, but she went down to the beach as often as before and took her solitary plunge just to show him that his company was not essential to her.

She had no way of knowing even if he knew of her lone swims or even if he missed her as much as she admitted to herself she missed him, but if it had not been for the fact that she saw Van every morning she would have felt terribly at a loss. As it was she found herself constantly looking round for the brown face with its wide grin, and the wet fair head bobbing up beside her.

At least on Sunday, she thought, she would have Van's company all day, but Sunday when it dawned was dark and miserable and she eyed the scudding clouds despairingly. Automatically her thoughts went to the unlikelihood of it being fit for sailing if the threatened storm broke and, for some reason, that cheered her somewhat. At least Gwyn would not be able to do much either.

'Are you seeing Van this morning?' her uncle asked, and she nodded, pulling a face at the weather outside.

'I am, but we shan't be able to do much in this.'

'English summer,' John quipped, and looked at her thoughtfully. 'Is Gwyn supposed to be sailing today?'

Sheena shrugged with what she hoped was an air of disinterest. 'I wouldn't know,' she told him, 'I haven't seen him since Monday.'

Her uncle's dark brows shot upwards in surprise. 'Monday?' he echoed, then nodded as if in understanding. 'I thought he'd been a bit grouchy all week, but I never imagined you two had quarrelled. What was it about, for heaven's sake?'

Sheena was reluctant to talk about it, suspecting that, inevitably, her uncle would see Gwyn's side rather than hers. 'I don't know,' she declared. 'Something silly.'

'Sweetheart, you must know,' he told her. 'People don't quarrel for nothing, especially you and Gwyn, you've known each other too long.'

'Perhaps that's the trouble,' Sheena declared, 'we've known each other *too* long. I object to being treated by him as if he was my – my big brother.'

John's dark eyes looked at her steadily for a moment and she could not be sure whether or not he was laughing at her. 'How do you want him to treat you?' he asked quietly, and something in his tone rather than his words brought a warm flush to her face so that she turned away hastily.

'Like a grown woman,' she said shortly. 'Is that asking too much?'

Her uncle sighed. 'Maybe you *have* known each other too long,' he said. 'Gwyn still can't forget you were a little girl, he coddles you too much.'

'Coddles me!' Sheena cried indignantly. 'He doesn't, Uncle John, he definitely doesn't.'

'I think he does,' her uncle argued adamantly. 'You run to him every time anything goes wrong for you, he's almost as much your guardian as ever I was when you were little, and he always does what you want to do. Oh, I know,' he added hastily when she would have denied it, 'he teases you and he makes a show of making you do as you're told, but in fact it's simply that nine times out of ten he knows your own mind better than you do. Why, he even kept last Sunday free because he knew Van Goalan wouldn't be here and you'd want company.'

'He couldn't see Cora anyway,' Sheena retorted, seeing herself on the losing side yet again, and her uncle shook his head.

'Sheena, you admitted yourself that he hadn't intended inviting her over even if she hadn't been going up to town.'

Sheena looked out at the rain and heard the wind squalling noisily round the house and lashing the sea into a fury of grey and white. 'Well, it won't do him much good if he *does* ask her over today, will it?' she said, not without a hint of satisfaction. 'They certainly can't go sailing in this weather.'

Her uncle, she thought, read more into her words than she intended and he chuckled softly as he shook his head. 'There *are* other things to do on a rainy day,' he told her, 'as I expect Van and you have discovered.' That was not, Sheena decided, an idea she liked to dwell on.

When Van came for her he seemed less dismayed than she had been by the weather, and the sight of his good-looking face smiling cheerfully did a lot to lighten her own mood. He kissed her briefly as he helped her into the car, then more lengthily after they were inside out of the rain.

'I thought we might run up to town,' he told her. 'It's not so inviting in the wide open spaces when it rains, is it?'

'It's a wonderful idea,' Sheena agreed, her eyes beaming happily, 'but I'll have to change. I can't go up to town dressed like this.'

He eyed her for a moment, then smiled. 'I don't see

why not,' he declared. 'You look perfectly all right to me.'

'Oh, Van! In a sleeveless cotton dress and no bag or gloves? I look like a country cousin, and I'd hate you to be ashamed of me.'

He leaned across and kissed her chin. 'All right, my darling, but make it quick, will you? Something dishy enough to send up every other man's blood pressure and turn them green with envy. Not that they won't be anyway,' he added as she slid out of the car again.

Sheena was so quick that her uncle blinked his disbelief when she reappeared completely transformed and she gave him a quick kiss and ran out to join Van again. 'Will I do?' she asked, and he smiled.

'Beautiful.'

'I haven't been to town for a long time,' she told him, 'I'm glad you had the brainwave.'

He seemed pleased at her reaction, but she could not help wondering as they drove along the coast road if it would have made any difference if she had not been so willing. Remembering her uncle's allegation that Gwyn always did what she wanted to do, she was ready to admit that Van was far less likely to do the same.

She sat back quite happily as the car sped along the motorway towards London, content despite the rain that still poured down relentlessly. In taking her up to London with him she felt Van was taking the first step in introducing her into his more usual environment and the idea pleased her enormously. It was as if he was already trying to make her part of his more customary way of life.

The pavements shone despondently grey and the lights from the shop windows as they drove through the West End made it seem as if it was already evening instead of morning.

'Lunch first,' Van decreed, turning the car into a side

124

street.

'I'm famished,' Sheena confessed with a wry smile.

'Good. There's a little Italian place I know just along here. Do you like Italian food?'

'Very much,' Sheena said. 'I know it's very bad for my waistline, but I can never resist it. Not that I have it very often, trips to town aren't very frequent and Sandlea doesn't run to Italian restaurants, not real ones anyway.'

'Oh, this is the real thing,' he assured her, 'and you'll like it.' He flicked a brief, teasing smile at her as they turned yet another corner into an even narrower street. 'If you like star-spotting you'll be in your element, only don't be too obvious, darling, or I'll never be able to go there again. Lots of professional people use it because it's possible to have a meal in peace without being recognized by fans and having to duck out quickly.'

She grimaced, reproachful about his jibe but prepared to admit the truth of it. 'I suppose I am unduly impressed by people in your profession,' she admitted, 'but I'm not *too* gooey-eyed, am I, Van?'

He shook his head, smiling. 'Did someone say you were?' he asked as if he suspected who the someone would be, but Sheena merely shook her head without answering.

The restaurant was very small and smelled delicious even from outside. Its atmosphere was quiet and relaxing and very Italian, so that she looked momentarily surprised when the romantic-looking, dark-eyed waiter betrayed a Cockney accent when he spoke.

'Nice to see you again, Mr. Goalan. Your usual table's free, I think.' He eyed Sheena appreciatively and gave Van a knowing smile as he led them to a discreetly placed table in a quiet corner.

'They know you here,' she said without thinking, and

added hastily, lest she should have been misunderstood, 'but of course you're known everywhere, aren't you?'

'Does it bother you?' He sounded genuinely interested in her answer and she was uncertain what it should be.

'No – no, not really, at least I don't think it does.'

The blue eyes smiled at her over the top of the menu while the waiter discreetly withdrew. 'But you find it a bit disconcerting?' he guessed, and covered her hands with one of his own. 'Don't let it trouble you, Sheena darling, a beautiful woman must get used to being at the centre of attraction.'

Sheena laughed, enjoying herself enormously and not least enjoying Van's flattery. 'Of course I'm not the centre of attraction,' she told him, although she was conscious of several curious glances from other lunchers, as if they wondered who she was. She knew that she was not the first woman he had ever taken out, that would have been naïve to expect so much, but the scrutiny of others gave her an oddly vulnerable feeling suddenly. A feeling she sought to hide by taking an interest in her surroundings.

Only two tables from theirs she recognized a well-known actor lunching with an incredibly lovely red-haired girl but, remembering Van's admonition that she must not be obvious about it, she tried to appear uninterested.

'Star spotting?' Van teased her, and she nodded, her eyes shining darkly at him, her mouth pouted softly at his teasing.

'Don't laugh at me,' she reproached. 'I'm not being all gooey-eyed, Van, but it's all so new to me. I promise not to look too much like a starry-eyed teenager, but that *is* Patrick Owen at the next table but one, isn't it?'

Van nodded, his eyes showing tolerant amusement. 'With his wife,' he agreed, 'they often come here too, and three tables behind you, only don't you dare turn around – and look, there's Richard Maxwell and Bridie Laughlan, they're regulars too. In fact everyone here almost is connected with show business in some way or other, that's why it's so popular. We can come here and not be stared at while we eat.'

'I promise not to stare,' Sheena told him with a smile, 'and I'm more than ready to eat.'

The food was excellent and swiftly and efficiently served by soft-eyed Italian waiters who seemed to anticipate their every wish. Probably, Sheena thought as she ate her meal, it was not only the privacy that brought all these people to such a tiny, out-of-the-way place to eat.

They had reached the coffee stage when a short stout man approached their table, his eyes inspecting Sheena with a shrewdness that was evident even behind the dark-rimmed, thick-lensed glasses he wore.

'Van, hello!' He had a pleasantly deep voice but with Cockney overtones and the shrewd eyes behind the lenses still looked at Sheena rather than at Van.

'Vince!' If Sheena had any doubts about Van's reaction to having his lunch interrupted, she was not long in doubt. He shook the other man by the hand and half rose from his chair, obviously pleased to see him, signalling to one of the waiters to bring another chair.

'I don't particularly want to break into your tête-à-tête,' he demurred. 'I can see you're not exactly seeking other company.'

'Oh, Sheena doesn't mind, do you, darling?' Her agreement was apparently taken for granted and she tried not to show the disappointment she felt at having a third member added to their party. 'Vince, I'd like you to meet Sheena Hastings, a near neighbour of mine in the wilds of Lea Bay. Sheena darling, this is Vince Garman.' Obviously, Sheena thought, sadly out of her depth, she was expected to recognize the name and she tried to put a hint of recognition into her smile when she shook hands.

The shrewd dark eyes looked at her speculatively. 'I see Van's taste in beautiful women is as impeccable as ever,' he remarked. 'Are you in our line of business, Miss Hastings?'

If she was not, Sheena felt, she would immediately go down in his estimation and she was prepared to admit her profession rather apologetically when Van forestalled her. 'Don't betray your aesthetic ignorance, Vince,' he laughed. 'Sheena's one of our better-known up-and-coming young painters.'

It was an extravagant claim for her modest successes, but she realized that in Van's world everything had to be slightly larger than life, and the little dark man certainly looked impressed.

'Forgive me,' he apologized, his grimace of regret deliberately exaggerated to make her laugh. 'I am, as Van says, an appalling ignoramus about anything outside show business, Miss Hastings. I hope you won't hold it against me.'

'Of course not,' Sheena smiled. 'I'm afraid Van's exaggerating rather, Mr. Garman. I have had some success with my paintings, but I'm not *very* well known, though I hope to be.'

'Aren't you the young lady who put Van on to this location he's got us all excited about?' he asked, and Sheena's heart sank at the mention of the one subject she did not want raised. She did not want to be reminded of what might happen to the place she loved so much, but she could not let Van see that, so she nodded, her smile a little uncertain.

'Have you got a decision yet?' Van asked eagerly, obviously having no such qualms. He offered an explanation to Sheena, his eyes having that bright, eager look she had seen there before when he visualized his own world in the lonely quietness of Barbell. 'Vince is directing the film,' he told her. 'As you know, he's the best director there is in this country, even in Europe,' he added extravagantly, 'and between us we intend sweeping the board, isn't that right, Vince?' The other man nodded, his smile understanding his star's enthusiasm. 'Vince knows it's you we have to thank for finding such a perfect spot,' he added. 'If only we can get permission to use it.'

Vince Garman shook his head slowly. 'It might be more difficult than we anticipated at first, Van,' he told him. 'Apparently they lay great store by their countryside in that part of the world and we've come up against some pretty strong opposition from the locals. They've already formed a sort of committee to fight us on the grounds of despoiling the amenities adjacent to their homes.'

It seemed not to occur to him that Sheena was one of the locals he referred to and she kept her eyes lowered while Van frowned over the news that all was not going well with his plans. 'Oh, damn it!' he declared. 'I might have expected something of the sort, I suppose, judging by Gwyn's reaction.' The other man looked his curiosity and Van explained, 'I'm staying with an uncle and a cousin, Gwyn's the cousin and he's one of the local business men. He's also determined to fight me tooth and nail over this, he said as much the other night, also he has a very persuasive tongue, so I believe, and he's as stubborn as a whole train of mules.'

'Can't they be persuaded, can't *he* be persuaded?' Vince Garman asked. 'We've offered a very substantial sum for the use of the place, that should have some effect, surely.'

Van shrugged. 'Coals to Newcastle,' he said. 'No one in Lea Bay is exactly poor and they're the nearest to the place, so it can't concern anyone else. Anyway,' he shrugged, as if he refused to be downcast by the setback, 'we'll have to see what can be done.'

It really mattered to Van, Sheena thought when the little man had left them, that he might not be allowed to use Barbell Sands as a setting for the film. He had set his heart on it and he would be a man who did not lightly relinquish anything he had made up his mind to have.

'I'm sorry, Van.' She put a hand to cover his, seeking in some small way to console him for his possible disappointment, and he smiled at her wryly.

'I can't lose a chance like this, Sheena, you do see that, don't you?' he said. 'I know I've made dozens of films and I don't exactly need this one to make my name, but – I don't know, somehow it's different. It'll be the greatest thing I've ever done and I *know* Barbell is the only place I can do it as I want to do it. Can you understand that?'

Sheena nodded. 'I think so,' she said softly.

He sighed deeply and touched her fingers one by one as he held her hand across the table. 'If Gwyn really is at the bottom of this core of resistance,' he said thoughtfully, 'maybe you could help.'

'Help?' Sheena thought she understood and she did not very much like it.

'Mmm.' He kissed her fingers gently. 'Maybe you could persuade him to change his mind, hmm?'

Trying to smile and look flattered, Sheena thought, was not easy when her heart and her mind were rebelling against the idea of deliberately trying to coax Gwyn out of something he believed in so earnestly, and she wished Van had asked her anything but that.

CHAPTER EIGHT

WHATEVER her feelings might have been about Gwyn's behaviour towards her at their last meeting, Sheena could not see herself doing as Van suggested. Not, she told herself ruefully, that she would be given the opportunity now, since he seemed to be avoiding her. It had occurred to her that perhaps he was seeing Cora Lindsey in the evenings instead, but she had noticed his car still in the drive when she had been for evening walks. Mostly it was at a time too late to start out and too early to end an evening with an attractive woman.

In a moment of speculation, later on the Sunday evening, she had tried to imagine herself enveigling Gwyn into changing his mind, but the necessary manoeuvres involved to achieve it seemed inevitably intimate and deceiving and she had dismissed the idea hastily.

She and Van drove to Barbell Sands the following morning and it was as fine and sunny as ever again, the only sign of yesterday's rain a freshness in the dusty leaves and a slight sponginess underfoot in the turf.

'Why couldn't it have been like this yesterday?' Sheena asked as they sat down in their favourite spot on the beach.

Van laughed. 'You must have rain sometimes, darling, and you didn't mind the change too much, did you?'

'Of course not,' Sheena admitted. 'I thoroughly enjoyed it, though I'm not really a town bird at heart.'

'That's a pity,' Van remarked, eyeing her speculatively. 'You're wasted on the wide open spaces, my darling, there's no one to show you off to.'

Sheena smiled, her eyes teasing him, though her question was more serious than it appeared. 'Is that why you took me up to town yesterday?' she asked. 'Just to show me off?'

'Why not?' he countered. 'I may have things going my way at the moment, but it never did anyone any harm to be seen with a beautiful woman. It's letting the crowd see that I can still have the pick of the bunch, sort of rubbing it in.'

A smile took the edge off the remark, but the sentiment did not altogether please her. She supposed, however, that it was a compliment in a way, if a rather impersonal one. 'I'm flattered,' she declared, determinedly light-hearted, and he turned and looked at her for a moment in silence, his eyes oddly expressionless, as if he was thinking of something else.

Then he smiled slowly in the way that always set her heart hammering uneasily. 'You don't need flattery,' he said softly, and bent his head to kiss her gently beside her mouth. 'Sheena!'

By now she knew what would happen and she half-closed her eyes even before she felt his mouth on hers and the dizzying, pounding sensation as the blood raced through her body. She knew too that she would experience that small tinge of disappointment when he released her, as if there was something missing from a kiss that promised so much. It always happened and, when she thought about it at all, it puzzled her.

He looked down at her shining dark eyes and the softness of her mouth and smiled. 'It's the magic of this place,' he told her softly. 'That and the way you get into my blood, my darling, it never fails.'

Reminded of what could happen to spoil that magic Sheena lowered her eyes. 'The magic of Barbell Sands,' she said, a hint of sadness in her voice that she sensed made him frown.

'I must come here alone some time,' he told her, 'and see if it acts in the same way, but I'm sure it will. It's a terrific atmosphere and perfect for *Man Alone*. That's the name of the film we're making,' he explained. 'You can see how even the title fits in, can't you? We *must* get that permission to make it here, Sheena, it's so perfect for it.'

'It's perfect for just doing nothing,' she told him with a hint of reproach. 'You said you loved the isolation and the feeling of timelessness about it, Van. Do you realize you'll probably lose all that with your technicians and extras here? It won't be the same.'

He raised himself on to one elbow and looked along the length of the beach. At the glitter of the sea and the dune grasses, heavier now with yesterday's rain and more servile than ever before the wind. 'It'll be the same for me,' he told her confidently.

She smiled up at the tanned, good-looking face above her and traced the slightly full curve of his mouth with one finger. 'Then I hope you won't be disappointed,' she said softly.

'I hope not.' He studied her for a moment with a speculative look in his eyes that she found a little disturbing. 'Darling.' He kissed her lightly on the tip of her nose. 'You *could* help, remember I asked you?'

'Help?' She looked anywhere but at him.

'Make sure the opposition isn't too serious,' he told her.

'But – but I don't see how I can,' Sheena objected, wishing he had not raised that subject again. After all her heart-searching she still could not bring herself to liking the idea at all.

'The locals, Vince said,' he reminded her, 'and that means Lea Bay, there's no one else within miles. It means your uncle, Uncle George, and most of all Gwyn.'

'There are others,' she declared, 'and I can hardly do anything about them.'

'I'm prepared to bet anything that Gwyn is the leading objector in this committee thing they've organized,' he told her. 'He knows Barbell and he thinks he has some personal claim on it, it seems to me. He feels very strongly about it.'

'As I do,' Sheena reminded him.

He kissed her again, his blue eyes glowing, not only with admiration this time but also with determination, she recognized, and so confident of her support. 'But you're on *my* side,' he insisted.

'I'm – I'm not sure I am,' Sheena demurred, wondering how much she was risking by crossing him on this point, but he appeared quite unconcerned and merely smiled and brushed his lips against her throat.

'Of course you are, my darling.'

'But—'

He laughed softly. 'You tackle Gwyn in your own sweet way. Talk to him, my sweet, make him change his stubborn Welsh mind and see reason.'

'But it may not *be* Gwyn,' Sheena argued desperately.

'It's Gwyn,' he assured her with a grim smile. 'He's formed that damned committee with the express intention of stopping me – us having the use of this place. He said he'd use every means he knew to stop me and he will.'

Sheena could well believe it, knowing Gwyn, but she was not yet prepared to do as Van wanted her to, not even for him, although she knew that sooner or later, inevitably, she would weaken. The worst part of it was that she felt as if she was betraying Gwyn by not coming out firmly on his side. Only it was so difficult to desert

Van when he took her support so for granted, and in something that was seemingly so important to him.

'I – I doubt if he'll listen to me,' she said, and he laughed.

'Of course he will.'

'But I haven't seen him for over a week.'

'You haven't?' He eyed her for a moment. 'Did you quarrel?' Sheena nodded. 'Dare I venture a guess – about me?' She nodded again and he kissed her gently and with a look of genuine regret in his eyes. 'I'm sorry, darling, I'm truly sorry. You've been friends for so long, haven't you?'

'Perhaps too long,' Sheena agreed, remembering her uncle's remarks on the subject. 'He still treats me as if I was eleven years old.'

'Poor darling!' The expressive blue eyes swept over her from head to toe in a way that brought the blood rushing to her face. 'He should open his eyes wider.' One long finger traced the curve of her mouth and he smiled.

'It's just that he never takes me seriously,' Sheena complained. 'Even my painting he teases me about as if – as if I was just a childish dabbler.'

He kissed her again, lightly on one cheek. 'Shame on him,' he said, 'and you a famous artist too!'

She pouted, suspecting he was teasing her too. 'I don't claim to be famous,' she denied, 'but I *am* a serious artist and I've done quite well so far.'

'Of course you have,' he consoled her. 'You're good enough to capture Barbell Sands on canvas, aren't you?' He frowned at her in mock severity. 'You haven't even started on my painting yet, have you?'

'Not yet,' she sighed, turning her head to look at the scene beyond them. 'I must start soon.'

He tapped her on her chin with one finger. 'Start tonight,' he told her. 'No more excuses, the evenings are still long enough for you to see and there must be an even better atmosphere here towards night.' He smiled at her. 'You're not scared of the dusk, are you?'

'Of course I'm not, though I've never been here in the evening before.' She nodded, firmly decided. 'All right, I'll start tonight after dinner, I'll still have about an hour of light left, I suppose.' She looked again along the length of the beach. 'I imagine it will be pretty effective when the light's going and the wind gets up even more,' she mused, then shivered slightly. 'I probably *shall* be scared, my imagination works overtime in a situation like that, but I'll come.'

As it happened dinner was over conveniently early that evening and John Cameron looked mildly surprised when Sheena got up from the table in far more haste than usual.

'Are you off somewhere?' he asked, and Sheena nodded.

'I promised Van I'd start on his painting of Barbell tonight and the light will be going soon.'

Her uncle looked surprised. 'You're doing a painting for him?'

'I am. He asked me to, the first week he was here.' She looked at her uncle's doubtful face appealingly, guessing he would have discussed the proposed use of Barbell Sands with Gwyn. In all probability he was on the committee that Van had talked about, although he had said nothing to her about it, something which hurt rather. There was no doubt that he would come out firmly on Gwyn's side in the argument and so perhaps did not say too much to her. 'He really loves Barbell, Uncle John, as I do,' she insisted. 'I know it's hard to believe when he's talking of using it as a location for a film, but – well, you just don't understand him.'

'I'm prepared to admit that,' John allowed dryly. 'If he feels so much for a spot like Barbell how can he want to ruin it by having it overrun with all the hotch-potch of his profession? Its isolation is its main appeal, and he's proposing to finish that for good and all.'

'Not for good and all,' Sheena denied, wishing she could sound more convincing, 'it's only for a – a few weeks.'

'A few weeks?' Her uncle eyed her shrewdly, suspecting her true feelings, she guessed. 'You don't believe that, sweetheart, any more than I do. Van Goalan may have fooled himself, or he may not care, but once the publicity surrounding that film has been released and – *absorbed* by his fans, they'll be swarming all over the place and you know it.'

Sheena did know it, but she was not prepared to admit it, so she merely shook her head. 'It may not happen if Gwyn has his way,' she said. 'Now please forgive me, Uncle John, I'd like to catch what light there is left, and I have to drive over there yet.'

A shrug accompanied by a mildly reproachful look were all that answered her and she went out of the room feeling more sorry for herself than ever. No one, it seemed, was prepared to understand Van's motives but herself and it gave her a strangely lonely feeling.

She was preoccupied as she drove the short distance to the sands, but soon absorption with the proposed painting helped lighten her mood and she almost forgot everything else. It would be best, she decided, to try and capture a view that encompassed all the characters of the scene at once, something suggestive of the character of the place rather than a strictly accurate copy.

There was the long sweeping infinity of the sand and sea and the waving grasses that somehow lent an added air of loneliness with their heads bowed and the soft whispering sighs they made in the wind. She had brought only a sketch pad tonight, with the object of making a few rough outlines, trying to get the composition of the picture in her mind before committing herself to canvas.

She remembered her half serious statement that her imagination would run riot here in the evening and felt a light flick of uneasiness as she sketched busily. She had never been here so late in the day before and she was surprised how different it looked. Or perhaps it would be more accurate to say that it looked the same but everything was exaggerated.

The sky had a dull, gold heaviness that gave an even more unreal look to the familiar scene. It had an air that affected her even more than the more reassuring daylight hours did and she sat for some time, a minute figure on the vastness of the sands, letting the atmosphere flow over her until she felt she could reach out and touch it.

Her dark head bent over the sketch pad, her fingers moved rapidly, chasing the ever-changing shadows and shapes that moved endlessly with the dying sun. The sea shifted and shone like liquid gold and for a moment she thought she saw some alien movement on its surface, a movement that held her still for a moment while she sought its origin but found none.

Her head bent again as she swept curves and ripples into a picture that constantly changed as her eyes found new shapes, and it was only when she raised her head to look again at the scene that she saw an addition that widened her eyes and caught her breath in her throat. She sat frozen still with unreasoning fear for a moment until she recognized the truth of what she saw, even then her eyes did not focus quite correctly and her heart was thudding wildly.

'Gwyn!'

She could not, she felt, have mistaken the tall, glistening body as he emerged from the water and strode up the beach some fifty yards from where she sat. The familiar gesture of combing his fingers through his hair confirmed her identification but did little to ease the tension in her as she watched him. He must, she thought, have been coming here instead of swimming from Lea Bay as usual. Rather than be in her company he had come here and sought the isolation of the sands.

She had become so absorbed in the atmosphere she was seeking to recreate that she felt like a watcher who has stumbled on to something outside his normal ken and without knowing why she hoped he would not see her there. She felt very small and vulnerable on the vastness of the sands and her hands became still again as she watched him, some deep, indefinable emotion stirring in her at the sight of the lone figure that seemed to blend so perfectly with the rest of the scene.

Almost instinctively, after a moment, she began to sketch in the figure of the man, the strong muscular body that seemed so much part of the uncanny atmosphere of the place. So much part of it that to Sheena he seemed suddenly as remote and timeless as his surroundings and she felt a heavy, dizzying throb in her pulse like a warning.

It was when she saw him striding on long legs across the sand towards her that she felt a sudden surge of panic that was neither logical nor characteristic, but wholly primitive. Perhaps because the light was already growing duskily indistinct and there was such an air of purpose in his stride, something in her responded to an age-old instinct to run.

Her sketch pad was clutched tightly to her as she ran along the cooling sand blindly, away from something she could not even guess at, nor attempt to define, her feet unaccountably clumsy over the wind-ruffled surface, pausing only when shortness of breath compelled her to.

Her long hair tumbled and falling about her face, she drew in great gasps of air and felt herself trembling. She did not turn her head to see if he had followed her, but sat down on the grass-ruffled edge of the dunes, trying to make sense of her own instinctive panic. She knew it was Gwyn, there was no doubt about it, but for a moment he had seemed to belong to another time, strange and remote, and she had been terribly afraid.

The light was going fast now and would not last much longer and the wind had risen, louder and more insistent as it blew in from the sea, rustling through the grasses and heightening the sense of loneliness. Sheena clasped the sketch book to her like a shield and shivered involuntarily, from something more than the chill of the wind. She must go back before it got too dark for her to find the car where she had parked it on the wide, expansive sameness of the common land behind the dunes. The moon was late rising tonight and no street lamps shone within a mile of Barbell Sands.

Walking along, just below the edge of the dunes she found it increasingly difficult to remember just where she had been sitting, for the light was all but gone now and the endless sameness of the sands and dunes defied distinction. Realizing at last that she was utterly and hopelessly lost, she stood still, looking at the faint, white luminescence of the tide to her right, feeling chillingly helpless in her isolation.

Her first thought was of Gwyn, but he would surely be gone by now, discouraged by her running away. He would have dressed and driven off, leaving her to her self-imposed loneliness. The only consolation she could offer herself was that her uncle knew where she had gone and would start a search for her if she was too late. In the meantime she was frighteningly and horribly alone in the silence and the night-cool wind and there was nothing she could do about the tears of frustration that rolled dismally down her cheeks.

She left the beach and went up on to the turf which at least felt warmer and less chilling than the sand, standing for a moment to try and get her bearings. There were no trees or lights that gave her a clue and all the gorse and other bushes looked dismayingly alike when she walked into them. Until the moon came up there would be utter and complete blackness.

She had been there, curled up beside a prickly gorse waiting for the light of the moon to help her, for perhaps ten minutes when she thought she heard a faint sound of an engine and caught sight of the brief yellow sweep of car headlights. She scrambled to her feet and saw them again. It *was* headlights, static now and comfortingly close, the long beams illuminating the bushes and shrubs for several yards, and Sheena began to run towards them.

The ground was far more uneven than she realized and she was impeded to a certain extent by the sketch pad that she still clutched to her, but she was so afraid that the lights would either go out or be driven off that she dared not slow her pace.

One careless step too many and she fell full length, the sketch pad under her, the breath knocked out of her by the impact, but at least she was on the edge of the circle of light and *some*one must have seen her.

For a second or two she lay there too winded to move, then hands lifted her up until she sat curled round and facing the lights, breathing erratically. 'I thought it must be you.' The voice was comfortingly familiar and so was the wry grin that commented on her dishevelled hair and dirty face, traces of tears still in her eyes. 'Only you could get yourself lost, then fall flat on your face when you're rescued!'

He was squatting on his heels beside her and Sheena

found it almost impossible to believe that it was the same man she had seen earlier, tall, bronzed and looking so completely unnerving. Now there was only the familiar brown face with its blue eyes regarding her, speculative and half-amused, and the wide friendly mouth crooked into a smile.

'Oh, Gwyn!'

He put his arms round her without hesitation when she buried her face against his chest and she felt as well as heard the chuckle that came from deep down. 'What on earth made you run off like that, you little idiot?' Gentle fingers smoothed her hair and she did not answer for a moment because she did not want to move.

'I – I was frightened,' she admitted at last, her voice muffled, and she felt him move as he reached down for the sketch pad.

'Of him?'

She looked at the strangely unfamiliar figure in the drawing and realized how perfectly she had captured the image of the man she thought she had seen. The muscular body, broad-shouldered and narrow-hipped, the angle of the head with its close, damp cap of hair, poised in mid-movement with the arms reaching out. She had not drawn in the towel he was reaching for and the posture seen as it was had an animal, primitive look that even now made her shudder but at the same time disturbed her strangely.

'It's – it's what I saw – thought I saw,' she amended hastily, and he laughed, a warm, deep and satisfyingly familiar sound.

'I'm not surprised you ran,' he commented. 'But I never realized I looked quite so much like Neanderthal man. I'm not sure I'm flattered.' He studied the sketch for a moment in the headlights' beam, an expression of surprise and understanding flicking across the rugged face briefly. 'It's damned effective though, Tuppence. I hope you'll use it.'

He helped her to her feet while Sheena considered the idea of Van's possible reaction to the inclusion of his cousin in the painting, especially in such a role. 'I don't think I can,' she told him, eyeing the stark black and white of the crude half-formed picture thoughtfully.

He opened the passenger door of his car and saw her in and it was not until he slid behind the wheel ready to start that she remembered her own car. 'I can't quite remember whereabouts I left it,' she told him, 'it all looks so much alike in the dark. Anyway, it shouldn't take long to find it with the car lights to help.'

'Nothing doing,' Gwyn retorted, starting the engine. 'I don't mind searching for lost girls in the dark, but I draw the line at cars. You can pick it up tomorrow morning, I expect you'll be here.'

She did not insist or argue, nor did she disagree that she might be there again tomorrow, but it did remind her that Van had enrolled her help in persuading Gwyn to change his mind about blocking the project to use Barbell Sands. At the time she had thought it unlikely that she would be able to get near enough to Gwyn to raise the subject, but now it seemed the way was open to her she found herself even more reluctant to talk about it.

They drove along the road back to Lea Bay in silence for a while. 'How did you find me?' she ventured at last, and he laughed.

'I didn't, you found me, remember?'

'You know what I mean,' she told him.

'I know. Actually I thought you'd fled for home when you went off like that, then I saw your car wasn't on the drive when I went past, and it still wasn't there when I looked a little while afterwards, so I came to see what you'd got yourself in to.'

'I see – thank you.' There seemed little else she could say and she was only thankful that he did not ask for more detailed explanations for her behaviour. Perhaps because he really did believe she had been frightened of him as he appeared in the drawing.

'You're welcome.' She could guess he was laughing at her, but she felt disinclined to quarrel with him about it.

'Have you been swimming there in the evenings?' she asked instead, as they turned on to the sea road at Lea Bay. She saw her opportunity for mentioning Van's business rapidly slipping away, but there was little she could do about it now.

She could just distinguish the white flash of his smile against the brown face before he turned his head again. 'I thought it was more tactful,' he told her.

'Because – because you knew I'd be on the beach?'

'Uh-huh.'

'And you wanted to avoid me?'

'You could say so,' he agreed, 'though not in the way you mean.'

She said nothing while he drove up to her uncle's house and stopped the car at the front steps. 'What other way is there?' she demanded, and he grinned.

'If you must know I didn't trust myself not to put you across my knee and wallop some sense into you, and I didn't think *that* would be a popular move with anybody, especially with you.'

So much for Van's hopes of her influencing Gwyn to change his mind, Sheena thought ruefully. He was as adamant as ever and any mention of Barbell Sands in that connection would probably only make him more stubborn. She knew Gwyn only too well, or she had thought she did, now the memory of that strange, frightening man on the sands still stayed firmly in her mind and refused to be dismissed or explained.

The front door opened as they got out of the car and her uncle appeared with Suna, smiles of relief on their faces when they saw her. 'Where did you find her?' John asked, and Gwyn grinned at him.

'Cowering under a bush by Barbell Sands,' he told him, and Sheena prepared to object to the exaggeration.

'Cowering under a bush?' her uncle echoed, while Suna came and took her hands, her grey eyes gentle and anxious.

'Sheena dear, what *did* happen?'

'She ran away and was hiding,' Gwyn told her before Sheena could put it into words that made sense. He held the sketch pad before him, studying the drawing, and Sheena wished uneasily that he would leave the explanation to her. 'From him,' he added, thrusting the pad at her uncle.

For a moment her uncle studied the stark explicit drawing and a curious Suna joined him, looking over his arm at the pad, then John's dark eyes flicked to Gwyn as if in understanding. 'I see,' he said quietly.

'It's a quite fantastic piece of work,' Suna declared with professional assurance. 'Quite remarkable, Sheena, and very revealing.'

'Very,' Gwyn echoed with a wry grin, again before Sheena could speak for herself. 'I'm not sure I like being stripped down to my soul like that, though. It's – it's almost indecent!'

'It's what I *saw*,' Sheena insisted, her cheeks flaming with colour as three pairs of eyes looked at her. 'I don't know what you're all making such a fuss about.'

'Don't you, darling?' Gwyn asked softly, and with such a look in his eyes that Sheena snatched the sketch book from him and held it against her defensively.

'I can't help it if you look like – like something from

the Stone Age,' she told him. She held the book away from her, eyes thoughtful. 'I think it has a – a sort of – of beauty,' she added softly.

'Oh, it has,' Gwyn agreed quietly. 'That's just what makes it so remarkable, Tuppence; as Suna said, it's very revealing.'

Sheena looked from one to the other, uneasy and on the defensive, and it was Gwyn who made the first move when he put an arm round her shoulders, smiling reassuringly. 'Don't worry about it,' he advised. 'Put it away somewhere for now, darling, and some day you'll realize what you've done.' He dropped a gentle kiss on the very tip of her nose and laughed softly. 'I'd better go, I promised Pop I'd join him in a game of chess and I've lost half the evening already. Not that it hasn't been well spent,' he added, and left Sheena more puzzled than ever.

CHAPTER NINE

VAN was much less sympathetic than Sheena expected when she told him about her getting lost the night before. He seemed far more concerned to know whether she had said anything to Gwyn about seeing his point of view over Barbell Sands and, when she had to confess that she had not even mentioned it, he seemed quite put out. In fact, in a less charitable frame of mind, Sheena would have said he was sulky about it.

They went to the sands, as Gwyn had guessed they would, and they swam and sunbathed as usual, but it seemed to Sheena that he was fractionally less attentive than usual and there was an absent air about his kisses that was rather discouraging, so that she felt rather let down and genuinely welcomed the reappearance of Gwyn that evening.

'Welcome back.' She thought it was safe to tease him, although he glowered at her in mock severity when she smiled.

'Don't take liberties,' he warned.

Sheena pulled on her cap, more relieved than she was prepared to admit to have their relationship back to normal.

'Race you in!' she challenged, and ran off down the beach, her long slim legs just holding the lead until he splashed into the water only inches behind her.

It seemed much longer than a week since they had quarrelled and he had stridden off so angrily, but she had not quite realized until now just how much she missed these lazy evening dips, even their almost childish bickering that usually came to nothing serious. The evenings were growing shorter much more quickly now and it was while they walked back up the beach that she realized there was very little of the summer season left.

There was always a certain sadness about this time of year, but this year there was more reason for her to feel slightly nostalgic. Hugging her knees, with her long dark hair half-hiding her face, she looked out at the brassy-looking sea and thought of what she would do when she was at last obliged to leave Lea Bay and all the things she knew so well and took for granted. Even Gwyn.

She looked at the brown, rugged face from behind the curtain of her hair and wondered what it would be like without Gwyn. Of course there would be Van and their life together. The excitement and glitter of his so different world, a world she would have to learn to live in, no matter how strange and unreal it seemed to her now. And perhaps, one summer season, Van would be appearing again in Sandlea and she could come with him and stay with Uncle John and Suna, perhaps visit Uncle George and Gwyn.

Gwyn and Cora. The two names came persistently into her mind together and she looked at him again through the concealment of her hair, wondering how serious he was about Cora. She took up a handful of sand and trickled it through her fingers as she spoke, not looking at him.

'Are you sailing on Sunday?'

He guessed, she thought, that there was more behind the question than just idle curiosity and he did not answer immediately. 'Why?' he asked quietly at last. 'Are you volunteering?'

She looked up then and found his gaze disconcertingly steady, only a hint of curiosity in it. 'I'd love to,' she confessed almost without thinking, 'but—'

'Then I'll sign you on.' He might have been treating it

all very lightly from the way he spoke, but she knew he wasn't and hated herself for having brought it this far only to let him down.

'I – I can't, Gwyn.'

His brows rose, comment enough without the cutting words that followed. 'Still getting your priorities right, eh? Cousin Van has first call on your time.'

'I've already promised, Gwyn, honestly. I *am* sorry, no matter what you think, but I can't – I mean—'

'You mean I'm still getting the old heave-ho in favour of the big star,' he told her dryly. 'Well, don't worry, Cora's coming over anyway.'

'Then – then you don't need me.'

He held her gaze for a long moment. 'I didn't say that,' he told her softly, then crooked his mouth into a smile. 'I can always use a standby crew.'

'You didn't sail last Sunday,' she said, trying to restore normality, 'let's hope it's better weather for you this week.'

'No, I didn't,' he agreed, drawing patterns in the sand with one finger. 'For one thing the weather was too bad, as you say, and for another Cora had a date in town, something which I'm sure you're speculating like mad about.'

Sheena looked at him uneasily. She had never said a word to him about seeing Cora with the man in the car, but she had mentioned it to Van. Perhaps rather rashly in view of their present state of relations. 'Should I be speculating?' she asked cautiously.

He raised his head and looked at her steadily. 'I thought maybe you'd seen her while you were in town with Van. I know it's a bit like a needle in a haystack, but it's possible, and you saw her before at Lea Point, didn't you?'

Sheena found it hard to meet his eyes. She had asked

Van not to say anything to Gwyn, but perhaps he had been provoked beyond discretion, Gwyn could be very annoying. It was the idea of him having done it in sheer malice that she dismissed hastily. She refused to think that Van would ever do anything so spiteful without extreme provocation.

'I – I wasn't going to tell you I'd seen them,' she insisted, appealing to him to believe her, and he grinned as if it mattered to him not at all.

'Cousin Van wasn't so reticent,' he told her, 'as you've obviously guessed.'

'I didn't – I mean I know *some*one must have told you, but—'

'You hoped it wasn't Van,' he finished for her. 'Oh lord, girl, your faith in humanity is touching.'

Sheena bit her lip, hoping he was as uncaring about it as he appeared to be. 'I'm sorry, Gwyn,' she told him. 'You needn't have known.'

'Not to worry, darling, Cora's life is her own affair,' he informed her airily. 'I don't keep tabs on her.'

'Oh, I see.'

He laughed softly and leaned over to kiss her cheeks lightly before pulling her to her feet. 'I'll bet you don't,' he retorted. 'Come on, it's time we went in.'

Sheena realized as they walked up the beach that she still had not done or said anything to try and persuade him in Van's favour over Barbell Sands. Looking up at him now, at the strong face and its firm jaw, she was as convinced as ever that nothing she or anyone else said would make him change, but Van expected her to try and some vague plan half-formed in her mind when he turned his head and looked down at her.

'Are you going anywhere interesting tonight?' she asked, trying to sound as casual as she could.

His eyes were both shrewd and curious and a wry smile

crooked his mouth for a moment before he spoke, as if he sought a reason behind her question. 'That has all the earmarks of an invitation,' he told her, and Sheena flushed at having her manoeuvre so easily interpreted.

'I – I didn't—' she began, but he cut her short with a laugh, taking her hand in his and holding it tightly.

'Oh, don't back out now, Tuppence,' he told her. 'I don't mind playing it your way.'

'Playing what?' Sheena asked, blinking.

'The old story of boy meets girl,' he told her solemnly. 'You know the idea.' He drew a deep breath and began chewing like someone masticating chewing gum, the most awful leer on his face as he leaned over her. 'Say, are you doin' anything tonight, beautiful?' The accent was pseudo-American and quite terrible and Sheena frowned over it.

'I wasn't—' she began, and he sighed.

'I see. Boy meets girl, girl plays hard to get,' he said, then grinned. 'And we all know she doesn't mean it.'

'Gwyn, stop it!' She shook her hand free and would have hurried off and left him, her face flaming with something more than embarrassment.

'Oh, come on!' He was beside her again in one long stride, his still damp head bent over her persuasively, and for some reason she was reminded of the way he had appeared to her on the sands last night. He held her by an arm this time and his grip was strong enough to hurt, as if he restrained either impatience or anger. 'Stop playing games, Sheena!' He brought her to a halt, his right hand joining the other in holding her still, a hard and totally unfamiliar glint in his eyes, so that she felt her heart skipping uneasily and a warning shiver trickle along her spine, just as it had last night.

'Don't, Gwyn!'

For a moment she thought he would lose his temper

with her, but after a few seconds he eased his grip and laughed, burying his face briefly in her dark hair. 'Oh dear, poor old Tuppence, you *do* suspect me of some ulterior motives, don't you? All I want to do is ask you to have supper with me and go dancing. Will you?'

Sheena did not answer for a moment, looking at him with wide dark eyes, still uncertain, then she nodded, managing a smile that earned her a brief kiss on her forehead. 'I'd love to, Gwyn, thank you.'

'About eight o'clock?'

Sheena turned his wrist and looked at his watch. 'That doesn't give me much time,' she complained, not too seriously. 'I'll have to change in a hurry and my hair will have to take pot luck.'

He laughed, lengthening his stride and pulling her along with him until Sheena called a halt, breathlessly, at the gate. 'Leave it loose,' he told her, grabbing a handful of her hair. 'I like something I can get hold of in case you try to run off.'

Sheena had seldom got ready for a date so quickly or with such anticipation, she realized as she took a last look at herself in a long mirror. There had been no time to do anything more than brush her dark hair until it shone like silk and hung loose about her shoulders as Gwyn had suggested. A rather pretty jade green dress flattered both her colouring and her figure and she thought she had done as good a job as possible in the time available.

She was already part way down the stairs when the door bell rang, and Mrs. Goodenough smiled at her approvingly on her way to admit Gwyn. He pursed his lips in a not quite silent whistle of approval and held out a hand to her as she came down the last couple of steps.

'Instant miracles,' he said, and raised the hand he held to his lips in a gesture that was more characteristic of Van.

'I'm glad you approve,' Sheena told him, feeling oddly shy, considering it was Gwyn.

'Are you ready?' he asked. 'Or do I have to wait while you gather up numerous O's and S's en route?'

'No O's and S's,' Sheena declared, already at the front door. 'I'm ready whenever you are.'

He grinned as he held the door open for her. 'From beachcomber to glamour girl in—' He consulted his watch with a serious frown. 'Just about twenty minutes,' he declared. 'Congratulations, Tuppence.'

'Beachcomber!' She glared at him in mock reproach as he saw her into his car and slammed the door after her. 'I looked no worse than you did.'

She always thought Gwyn looked his best in casual clothes, but she had to admit he looked very smart and presentable in a light grey suit and tie, a white shirt showing off his tan flatteringly. 'We're going to the Canna Club,' he informed her as they drove out on to the road. 'I tell you that now,' he added with a swift grin, 'before you start asking a whole lot of questions.'

'I had no intention of asking a whole lot of questions,' Sheena denied indignantly, but a moment later, curiosity got the better of her and she looked at him questioningly. 'Why the Canna Club?' she asked, and he laughed.

'Questions, questions! Why *not* the Canna Club?' he countered.

'Because,' Sheena said slowly and not without satisfaction, 'you've refused to take me there several times in the past because you said it wasn't – it wasn't suitable, whatever that might mean.'

'It means,' he told her, turning his head briefly, 'that you were too young at the time for the sort of atmosphere the Canna exudes from its unholy walls. Now I think it's time you saw a bit of the seamier side of life. You're a big girl now.'

'I'm glad you realize it,' Sheena retorted, feeling strangely elated and for no good reason she could think of except that his description intrigued her. 'I'm tired of you treating me as if I was still a five-year-old. I was beginning to think you'd overlooked the fact that I'm a grown woman.'

Again his head turned for a brief moment. 'I haven't done that,' he said quietly, and Sheena wondered if it was the almost dark interior of the car that made her see a deep glowing warmth in his eyes before he turned away again.

The Canna Club was situated away from the more family holiday atmosphere of the sea front at Sandlea and looked like nothing so much as a rather dilapidated brick barn from the outside. Inside it was small and dimly lit and the decor was crude rather than artistic, but it had an air about it that people revelled in without quite knowing why. What lighting there was came from red candles stuck into empty bottles, their flickering light casting dark, grotesque shadows on the plain yellow brick walls.

'It's – it's creepy,' Sheena whispered, staying close to Gwyn as they followed a waiter across the narrow room, but Gwyn merely smiled and squeezed her hand encouragingly.

Their table was set against one wall and allowed them to watch other couples who either sat at the tables or gravitated to the small area reserved for dancing and, after a while, Sheena found herself absorbing the rather bizarre atmosphere of the place and enjoying herself.

'Happier now?' Gwyn asked as they sat drinking a rather heady wine, the flickering candlelight throwing large, distorted versions of them both on the wall.

'It's different,' Sheena allowed, 'and I like it now I've got used to it. It gives everybody a slightly sinister look and makes me feel delightfully wicked.' She blew gently at the candle on their table, the yellow light darting shadows across her face and giving her darkness the look of a rather beautiful witch. 'Isn't it a bit of a fire hazard with all these candles?' she added, and Gwyn pulled a face at her.

'How romantic,' he taunted. 'Soft music and candle-light and she starts talking about fire hazards!' He leaned across the table, his rugged face looking darkly sinister with the hundred and one small shadows that betrayed a good bone structure and an unexpectedly deep cleft in his chin. His eyes more violet than their usual blue above the unsteady light. 'You look like some dangerous *femme fatale*,' he told her solemnly, 'and very beautiful.'

Sheena wished she could do something about the rapid and disconcerting pounding of her heart against her ribs and tried to concentrate on what she had planned to do. A *femme fatale*, he had called her, and it was unnervingly accurate in view of what she had in mind. Now was the opportunity she needed to try and persuade him to see Van's point of view, she would never have a better, but somehow she felt oddly reluctant to raise a subject that must inevitably cause controversy, and she hesitated.

He flicked her an inquiring look and waved a hand in front of her eyes. 'I said you looked beautiful,' he told her, 'and got no response beyond a blank stare into space. Are you as reticent with Cousin Van, I wonder?'

'Oh, Gwyn, please don't spoil it,' she begged, her mouth pouted reproachfully.

'By mentioning Cousin Van?' he asked in mock sur-prise, then covered her hand with his and smiled apolo-getically. 'I'm sorry, Tuppence. Would you like to dance?'

'I'd love to.'

Gwyn had taught her to dance and always felt that she

danced better with him than with anyone else, although she had never had the opportunity to try with Van. Her head just reached his breast pocket and his face rested against her hair as they went round the tiny dance floor.

'It's been a long time,' he said, and Sheena did not need to question his meaning. It *did* seem a long time since she had danced with Gwyn.

Mostly, since Van's arrival, she had stayed home in the evenings or gone for a walk and she had no idea what Gwyn did with his time unless he saw Cora Lindsey. She had been twice into Sandlea to see Van in the summer show at the Majestic and they had driven home together afterwards along the sea road in the moonlight. It had seemed very exciting and romantic to Sheena, but she wished they could have come dancing as she and Gwyn were now. It was unreasonable of her, she supposed, because he would be tired after the show and glad to get home and rest – but she could dream.

A tug at her hair made her look up sharply, her gaze indignant when she saw Gwyn's grin. His fingers still held her head back by her hair and she glared at him. 'I told you to leave it loose so I'd have something to get hold of in case you ran off,' he told her. 'You were well away, where were you?'

'Oh, you horrible brute, let go!' She reached up to free her hair and he let it go with a laugh.

'Where were you?' he insisted.

'Nowhere,' Sheena told him, and he shook his head slowly, obviously unconvinced.

'I can guess in one,' he told her. 'You were wishing I was Cousin Van and that it was his handsome face looking down at you in the gloom instead of my ugly one.'

'You're *not* ugly!' The denial was swift and indignant and for a moment he was quiet, looking at her steadily, the flickering shadows making all manner of changes in the rugged lines of his face.

'I shall kiss you for that,' he informed her solemnly, and made good the promise, slowly and gently, on her mouth, his arm tightening almost imperceptibly round her.

Sheena said nothing, but her legs felt suddenly weak and the pulse in her temple was almost blinding in its urgency. They neither of them spoke again until the music stopped and they made their way between the tables back to their own.

'More wine?' He held up the bottle invitingly, but Sheena shook her head.

'I mustn't,' she said. 'I'm already lightheaded, you know what I'm like.'

'You can't hold your liquor,' he agreed in that pseudo-American accent again. 'Well, this stuff isn't likely to send you on an orgy, darling, so have some more. I'll see you safely home if you should get squiffed, don't worry.'

Sheena eyed him in mock disapproval as he filled her glass. 'Where do you get such – such crude expressions?' she asked, her mouth set as primly as it was possible, and he laughed.

'Mixing in bad company,' he told her.

'I can believe it,' she retorted. 'You get worse.'

'Do I?' He looked surprised. 'Well, I keep the same company I always have – with one exception, of course.'

Sheena frowned her dislike of the allusion and she sipped her wine slowly, her eyes thoughtful. 'Gwyn, why don't you and Van get on together now? You seemed such good friends when he first came to Lea Bay.'

'The old adage?' he suggested. 'Like familiarity breeds contempt?'

'Oh no!' The harshness of it was unexpected and it

157

appalled her. For one thing it was so unlike Gwyn to be so bitter about anything, and she looked at him with worried eyes. 'It's – it's about that business at Barbell, isn't it?' she ventured.

For a moment he held her gaze, his eyes dark and shadowed in the guttering light. 'Not entirely,' he said quietly, at last. 'That was the culmination.'

Anything else but Barbell did not concern Sheena at the moment so she did not question his reasons. 'You – you still won't change your mind about it?' she asked, and knew from the stubborn set of his jaw that he wouldn't.

'Do you expect me to?' he asked, and she made a moue of doubt, watching him with wide, appealing eyes.

'I don't know,' she said softly, 'will you?' He shook his head. 'Not even to please me? If I ask you very humbly and earnestly to change your mind?' It was the first time she had ever begged him for anything like this. The first time she had ever attempted to use her wiles as a woman to make him do as she wanted and it gave her a strange sense of power when he did not look at her, but sat silent and tense as if he fought some inner battle with himself.

For a second, when he at last looked up, she detected a glitter of anger in his eyes and saw the fingers that were curled round his glass whiten at the knuckles. 'If I thought you were asking for the right reasons,' he said softly, as if he controlled his voice with difficulty, 'I'd withdraw my objections like a shot and come out on the side of the angels. But you're *not* asking because you want Barbell destroyed, Sheena, you're asking because Van told you to, you're miming *his* words, *he's* working the strings, and I'm damned if I'll be browbeaten by his puppet, however beautiful she may be.'

He swallowed a mouthful of wine, then emptied the glass in one go and his mouth crooked in to a smile when he looked at her again. 'Now I know why you look like a *femme fatale*, darling. You're working at being one and you're doing very well. Full marks!' He waved an airy hand. 'Keep up the good work. Who knows, next time you might succeed.'

It seemed unbelievable that it could be Gwyn speaking to her like that and for a moment Sheena stared at him blankly. 'Gwyn, I—'

'I *know* what you're up to, darling,' he interrupted, and she disliked the way he drawled the endearment and made it sound cheap, 'but it won't work. You and Van are wasting your time, and if that's what was behind that very inviting question about what was I doing tonight, I'm sorry to disappoint you.'

Sheena had never felt so small and humiliated in her life and she tried to find words to tell him so, but found them elusive. She shook her head slowly, unable to speak, and got to her feet, her legs trembling as if they would let her down as she walked quickly and half blind to the exit.

The air outside was cool and fresh after the close, smoky confines of the club and she leaned for a second or two against the wall at the corner of the car park. It might be possible to find a taxi, it was not too late, but it would mean walking into the town proper in search of one and she toyed with the idea of going back and asking the doorman to ring one for her. It was a temptation, but she relinquished the idea in case Gwyn had followed her out.

It was no use standing there, she decided after a moment; feeling sorry for herself would do her no good at all and she was horribly uncertain just who was most responsible for her state of misery – Gwyn or herself. At the moment she hated him intensely and wanted to put as much distance as possible between them.

There were quite a lot of people about still, most in holiday mood and some of them having obviously imbibed freely during the evening. Whistles of appreciation and a selection of complimentary but ribald remarks hastened her pace and she thought it had never seemed so far from one place to another.

Every step she took seemed to make her more miserable. Gwyn had absolutely no right to speak to her like that, no matter if he had guessed her motives correctly, she would tell him so as soon as she saw him again and had better control of her emotions. At the moment she felt very much like crying and the leers and cat-calls that followed her progress did nothing to help. She felt very vulnerable and very much alone and she would have loved to sit down somewhere and let the tears flow. A shoulder to cry on would have been very welcome at that moment.

She was taking a short cut down another street when a car pulled up alongside her and, despite her erstwhile hatred of him, her heart leapt hopefully at the thought of Gwyn having caught up with her. Nevertheless she walked on, chin high and a gleam of stubbornness ready in her eyes.

'Come on, darlin', get in.' She was totally unprepared both for the nasal twang of the speaker and for the hand that lay persuasively on her arm, and she turned wide, scared eyes to the man beside her.

He had obviously taken more drink than was good for him and so had the other two men who leered at her from the interior of the car drawn up beside the kerb with the door open invitingly.

'Let me go!' She tugged at her arm and the man grinned, tightening his hold as he tried to urge her towards the car.

'Gwyn!' The cry was instinctive and she saw the swift

flash of dismay on the man's face when he thought she was not alone after all.

She was scarcely aware of what happened next, only that her captor released his hold on her with unbelievable suddenness and fell back against the car with a satisfying thud, his eyes blinking stupidly.

'Get in and get going, fast!' She could hardly recognize the voice nor the face, so coldly angry, blue eyes glittering like ice in the street lighting.

There was no argument or hesitation on the man's part. He scrambled with more haste than dignity into the car and was driven off at well over the permitted speed limit, the door not quite closed behind him.

For a moment Sheena stared after it, her mind whirling chaotically with the speed of events, then she turned and looked at Gwyn. His face was still set cold in anger but already showing signs of relaxing slightly.

'When you're ready,' he told her, and held open the passenger side door.

'I—'

'Get in, Sheena.' She found she had little choice, for he bundled her into the car unceremoniously and slammed the door, then strode round to his own side, wearing an expression that brooked no argument.

He too drove off at a speed that must have been illegal, his profile stern and uncompromising. Not in the least encouraging and Sheena's heart sank.

'Thank you.'

As an attempt to heal the breach it was meek and not very hopeful, but to her relief he turned his head briefly and she thought there was a hint of smile at the corners of his mouth. 'You're welcome.'

'How – how did you know I—'

'Needed rescuing?' He laughed shortly. 'Easy,' he declared. 'For one thing you always need rescuing eventually from your own folly, and for another I followed you from the car park and kept you in sight. I'm surprised I wasn't pulled up by some sharp-eyed copper for loitering with intent, in which case you'd have to have fought off your admirers alone.'

Sheena shivered at the memory of it. 'I – I don't know what I'd have done.'

'Neither do I,' he admitted frankly, 'so thank your stars I took it into my head to follow you. I wanted to see what you'd do,' he added with more of his old style.

'I was going to get a taxi from the town centre,' she told him, and heard the short laugh that was not altogether amusement.

'You thought you'd put me in my place, did you?' He negotiated a corner. 'Well, I dislike having people walk out on me, Sheena, especially in a public place.'

'I'm sorry.' There was little else she could say and little enough encouragement for that. His brusque and rather ruthless manner was entirely new to her and he had called her Sheena at least three times tonight.

For several seconds he said nothing and she wondered if he was going to keep up his disapproval all the way home, then he turned his head briefly and one hand left the wheel for a minute to cover hers. 'I know you are,' he said softly.

She looked at the dark profile again, less forbidding now, his attitude less tense and angry. 'You *were* rude to me,' she ventured, unwilling to shoulder all the blame for the incident.

'For speaking the truth?' A brief flash of white betrayed a smile. 'You're very potent when you put your mind to it, Tuppence. It seems such a shame you've chosen a lost cause.'

Sheena flushed at the jibe and glared at him crossly. 'I don't know that it is a lost cause,' she retorted. 'And you

aren't the only person with a say in what goes on at Barbell Sands.'

'Maybe not,' Gwyn agreed, 'but I'm head of the committee to fight it, and I *will* fight Van and his film people
tooth and nail, make no mistake about that. I don't think
the rest will take too much convincing that I'm right.'

It was likely enough to leave Sheena in frustrated
silence and she said nothing more until they pulled up
outside the house and she turned and looked at him – a
long, searching, speculative look which he met straight-
faced. 'Why *are* you being so stubborn?' she asked. 'Is it
really because you care so much about Barbell?'

'Of course I care,' he said. 'Don't you?'

'Yes, you know I do, I've always loved it you know
that, but—'

'But you're ready to do anything because Van wants
you to,' he declared impatiently. 'Well, forgive me if I
differ, sweetheart. I'm not prepared to sell my soul – even
for love.'

CHAPTER TEN

SHEENA, not very hopefully, spoke to George Madoc about Barbell Sands a couple of days later and his reaction was not very encouraging. He looked at her with genuine regret and Sheena's heart sank.

'I'm sorry, Sheena dear,' he told her. 'I hate being ungallant enough to deny you *any*thing, but – well, I honestly can't do other than go along with Gwyn on this.'

'It's all right, Uncle George, it's only what I expected,' Sheena sighed.

Seeing her look of disappointment, he put a comforting arm round her shoulders as they stood together in the window of the sitting-room at the Madoc house. 'I'm sorry, my dear, I really am, but I can't change my mind now when there are so many of us in agreement. This committee that we've formed, you see, all the residents of Lea Bay have signed a petition without exception and, as I've joined them, I can't back down now and let them all down.'

'Gwyn formed the committee, didn't he?' Sheena asked, and George Madoc nodded.

'That puts me in an even more awkward position,' he added. 'Because we started the whole thing.'

'Gwyn started it,' Sheena insisted. 'But has it really been discussed properly, Uncle George? I mean really talked over, or did you all decide in the heat of the moment, without discussing it at all?'

George Madoc grimaced rueful admittance of the fact. 'I suppose we did, if I'm to be absolutely honest,' he told her. 'We were all rather het up about it and Gwyn can be a very convincing advocate, you know.'

'I know,' Sheena agreed wryly. 'That's exactly what I mean, though. Were you talked into taking such a firm stand by Gwyn rather than discussing it first and then making up your minds?'

George **Madoc** smiled ruefully. 'One could claim it was more a case of instant decision, encouraged by Gwyn, rather than careful consideration.'

'I thought so,' Sheena declared, and he looked at her and frowned.

'I can't quite understand why you're in favour of the scheme, Sheena, quite frankly,' he said. 'I always thought you liked Barbell the way it is.'

'Oh, I do, I love it,' Sheena insisted, 'but—'

He nodded his head, his eyes shrewd. 'It's because Van wants it, is that it?'

'Something like that,' Sheena agreed, wishing she felt more sure of herself, 'but it really isn't fair to just make a snap decision on Gwyn's say-so, Uncle George. The scheme means an awful lot to Van, you know.'

'And Van means an awful lot to you, hmm?'

Sheena felt the colour warm her cheeks and wondered how much Gwyn had said to his father. She nodded, in two minds whether to be as frank with him as she had been with Gwyn. 'I'm very – fond of him, Uncle George.'

He sighed and sat down in an armchair, signing her to another close to it. 'I suppose Van is the type of man who inspires girls of all kinds to have romantic dreams about him,' he said, 'but I thought you were different, Sheena. I hadn't imagined you indulging in such fancies.'

'It isn't a – a fancy,' Sheena insisted, rather surprised at his attitude. Perhaps he and Gwyn were more alike than she had realized.

He looked at her for a moment as if some realization had just dawned and she thought he looked less than pleased about it whatever it was. 'You mean you're serious about Van?'

Sheena nodded. 'Quite serious, Uncle George. I – I love him and I'm almost sure he loves me.'

'You're in love with him or you love him?' George Madoc asked, uncharacteristically pedantic, and Sheena frowned.

'I – I don't know the difference, I don't think,' she told him.

'That's what I thought,' he averred, nodding wisely. 'So many girls *don't* know the difference, but there is one, Sheena, quite a big difference.' He frowned thoughtfully. 'I hadn't realized things had reached that stage. Does – does Gwyn know?'

Sheena was rather at a loss to follow his reasoning, but she nodded. 'Yes, I told him, he's known for some time.'

'Ah!' Evidently that enlightened him further.

'He doesn't like Van,' Sheena declared. 'It's because of Van wanting to use Barbell for his film location, of course, he really dislikes him now. I'm sorry about it because they used to be quite good friends when Van first came, but Gwyn's being so – so stubborn about this and he just won't give in, not even just a little bit.'

George Madoc smiled wryly at the denigration of his son. 'You can't tell me anything about Gwyn's stubbornness, my dear, he's always had a mulish streak. As a child it earned him many a good hiding, but he never gave an inch.'

'I – I tried to persuade him,' Sheena confessed, 'but he wouldn't listen, he was just rude. He was so rude I walked out and left him.'

'Oh?' He looked interested.

Sheena nodded. 'It was on Tuesday night when he went to the Canna Club,' she said, pulling a face over the

166

memory of it. 'I was so furious with him, we quarrelled and I left him there.'

George Madoc made a wry face. 'He didn't say anything about that to me,' he said, 'but then he wouldn't. Gwyn's as proud as Lucifer, although he may not show it very often, especially to you.' He frowned suddenly and looked at her curiously. 'But he brought you home, surely, didn't he?'

'Oh yes, eventually,' Sheena agreed, 'and I was very glad to see him. He followed me,' she added by way of explanation, 'and he rescued me from some rather tipsy types who were – well, they were running true to form, I suppose.'

'Ah, I see. I couldn't quite see Gwyn leaving you to wander about Sandlea on your own at that time of night.'

'No, he wouldn't,' she agreed, then looked across at him hopefully and sighed. 'If only he wasn't so stubborn about this business,' she added, 'it wouldn't be so bad, but he just won't listen to reason. Maybe if you tried.' She widened her eyes and looked very appealing. 'Uncle George, you wouldn't change *your* mind, would you?'

He shook his head, but she thought he looked a little less certain than before. 'I'm afraid not, Sheena, much as I'd like to go along with you. It would spoil Barbell for good, you know, once the film people had been there.'

'It – it could be left exactly as it was,' Sheena insisted. 'There wouldn't be any permanent buildings put up and the novelty of it being a film location would soon wear off. You know how quickly people forget.'

'Hmm.'

He was definitely weakening, Sheena thought, and pressed home her advantage hastily. 'It's unlikely to attract crowds when they're filming because for one thing it will be early in the year and for another it's so far off the beaten track. It *is* the perfect background for the story they're doing, Uncle George, and Van wouldn't let them ruin it. He's as fond of the place as I am, or anyone else.'

He was silent for a moment while he regarded her curiously, then he smiled. 'He's chosen a very persuasive ambassador for the mission,' he told her.

'Persuasive enough?' Sheena asked, and he pursed his lips doubtfully.

'We'll see,' he demurred. 'It may be possible, I suppose, to compromise somewhere along the line.'

'Oh, Uncle George!' She left her chair and planted an enthusiastic kiss on his cheek. 'Thank you.'

George Madoc pulled a face. 'Don't thank me yet,' he told her. 'I haven't done anything and I may not be able to.'

'But you'll try?'

'I'll give it some thought,' he agreed, 'which is what we should have done in the first place, I suppose.'

'Well, at least it's a step in the right direction,' Sheena said, 'and that's something.'

George laughed ruefully as he looked at her pleased expression. 'I don't know what Gwyn's going to say,' he told her. 'He's all set for a no-holds-barred fight and if I just so much as suggest – ah well, I'll have to see.'

That evening at dinner Sheena, flushed with her success with Uncle George, thought she might well adopt the same tactics with her uncle and set about it with less apprehension than she had previously.

'But I don't understand you, Sheena,' John told her when she broached the subject. 'You profess to be very attached to Barbell and yet you're prepared to let Van Goalan and his minions swarm all over it. Don't you care about it any more?'

'Of course I care,' Sheena insisted, 'but it won't be as

bad as you seem to think, Uncle John.'

'I don't see that,' John argued, 'it *must* make a difference, anyone can see that.'

'Uncle George agreed that none of you had ever really discussed it,' she told him, and saw the quick frown of surprise that greeted the information.

'You've already spoken to George about it?'

'Yes, I have,' Sheena admitted, 'and he conceded that you mostly allowed yourselves, in the heat of the moment, to be influenced by Gwyn, and Gwyn can be very persuasive. It's the Celtic gift of the gab,' she added coarsely and in imitation of Gwyn, and her uncle cocked a brow at her.

'I'm beginning to realize Gwyn isn't the only one who has it,' he commented.

Sheena smiled. 'Admit it, Uncle John, you *were* rushed into a hasty decision, weren't you? You didn't really consider all the whys and wherefores of the matter before digging in your collective heels with Gwyn cracking the whip over you all to keep you in line.'

John laughed at the picture that conjured up. 'That's exaggerating a bit,' he protested, 'but to be perfectly honest I suppose it's partially true. All the same, it doesn't make Gwyn any less right about it.'

'But it simply isn't fair to just dismiss it out of hand without even discussing it,' Sheena objected. 'Admit I'm right on that at least, Uncle John.'

He nodded, smiling at her flushed face, eager face. 'I suppose you are,' he allowed, and Sheena felt a glow of elation at the admission, 'but it wouldn't be easy changing the decision now.'

'But you'll talk to them,' she urged, 'ask them to discuss it properly before being too final about it?'

'I'll try,' John agreed, 'though I'm not sure I should. We'd need to get some sort of written guarantee from the film people about restoration and that sort of thing. Loss of amenities is something we all have to consider very carefully these days, we lose so much without raising a finger to do anything about it.'

'But you wouldn't *be* losing it,' Sheena insisted, 'only lending it.'

'Hmm.' The dark eyes studied her for a moment, much as George Madoc had done. 'Goalan certainly knew what he was doing when he got *you* on his side, didn't he?'

'I – he didn't actually get me on his side,' Sheena demurred, but her uncle shook his head.

'Oh yes, he did,' he told her. 'Gwyn said so.'

'Oh, Gwyn!' She frowned, her eyes reproachful. 'Why is *Gwyn* always such a paragon of virtue? Van cares about Barbell as much as he does, only he's not so – so selfish about it.' She quieted suddenly, looking anxious. 'You will think about it, Uncle John, won't you? Talk to Uncle George and some of the others about it? I think *he* may change his mind in time.'

To her surprise her uncle laughed and hugged her tight. 'Oh, sweetheart, you *are* determined, aren't you?'

'As determined as Gwyn Madoc can be,' Sheena declared stoutly. 'We'll see who's most stubborn when it comes to a fight.'

Sheena did not see Gwyn that evening on the beach because for one thing it was much cooler than of late. With only a few days of August left the evenings were sometimes quite chill, although the weather was holding well and normally she was not cowardly about a lower temperature in the water. Another reason, though one she was less prepared to admit, was that she did not feel like facing Gwyn in case his father had told him of her part success in persuading him to see Van's point of view.

Saturday morning was bright and warm and Van came

for her as usual. They drove along the coast road as far as a small cove just the Lea Bay side of Sandlea. It was usually deserted except for the clamouring gulls that squabbled noisily at the water's edge.

'Darling Sheena!' He kissed her lingeringly as they walked round the curve of the sandy cove, out of sight of the road. 'Uncle George told me.'

'Told you?' For a second she was genuinely puzzled.

'About your powers of persuasion,' he reminded her, obviously delighted even with so minor an achievement.

'But he hasn't really changed his mind,' she demurred. 'Don't count your chickens, Van, it may come to nothing.'

He kissed the tip of her nose, his blue eyes glowing with satisfaction. 'I think it'll come to something,' he told her confidently. 'Gwyn was furious last night, but Uncle George still stuck fast to the fact that a lot of what you'd said was truth.'

'I spoke to Uncle John too,' Sheena told him, in two minds whether the idea of Gwyn being furious pleased her or not.

'Did he see reason too?' Van asked, and Sheena nodded.

'Only as far as Uncle George did,' she admitted, 'but it's a start.'

'It's marvellous progress,' Van enthused, then sighed deeply in satisfaction. 'Sheena, you've no idea how important this is to me.'

'I have,' Sheena said softly, 'that's why I've tried so hard.' She looked up at the tanned, good-looking face and smiled. 'Nothing's more important to you than your work, is it, Van?'

'Nothing,' he agreed unhesitatingly and rather dauntingly.

Sheena was silent for a while, thoughtful and a little wistful as they walked round the tiny cove to sit on a sheltered hump of rock. There was so little of summer left and the days passed so quickly, before she knew where she was it would all be over, and she hated living in this limbo of uncertainty. She loved being with Van and she had no doubt how he felt about her, although he had said nothing in so many words, but it was all right, she knew it was.

'What happens when you – when you fall in love?' she asked suddenly, hoping the question sounded as light as she tried to make it.

'In love?' The fair brows arched in surprise. 'Falling in love makes no difference at all, my darling. To me my job always comes first.'

'Always?' she echoed, and he nodded.

'Always.'

'Even when you – when you *really* fall in love with someone?' she insisted, and he laughed and hugged her close.

'*When* I do I'll let you know,' he said, and Sheena felt suddenly small and rather chill. He must be teasing her, of course, it was sometimes difficult to know. Perhaps he just took it for granted that she knew he loved her, the same way he must know how she felt about him although she had never actually said so. It was, so she had always heard, something one recognized instinctively.

'There isn't much of the summer left now,' she said, after a long silence, and he sighed.

'The summer season,' he mused. 'The time when anything is possible and everything seems slightly larger than life.'

'Does it?' Sheena asked, unsure that she liked the idea.

He kissed her and laughed softly. 'It does,' he insisted.

'It's the atmosphere of these holiday towns, something in the air and the freedom from everyday restrictions that sends everyone slightly crazy and makes a holiday romance seem like the big passion of a lifetime.'

'Sometimes they are,' Sheena ventured.

'Sometimes,' he agreed. 'Sometimes they are, my darling.' He kissed her, gently at first, then more passionately until Sheena's head spun dizzily, only that small and inevitable flick of disappointment lingering when he released her. 'But not always,' he added softly.

'Van—'

'Ssh!' He silenced her again and it was only when the faint murmur of voices reached them, vaguely at first, that Sheena realized they were about to be discovered and drew away.

'Someone's coming,' she told him, and he frowned.

The voices were soon louder and a moment later two people walked into view. The cove was sufficiently small for one of them to be instantly recognizable to Sheena, and to Van too, apparently, for he pursed his lips in a silent whistle.

'Well, well, the fair Cora.' He cocked a questioning brow at Sheena. 'Is that the same man you saw her with before, Sheena?'

'I think so.' She frowned, taking only a cursory glance at the couple, her colour high with embarrassment as they walked nearer, far less concerned than she was at seeing them there.

'Hello, Sheena!' A friendly wave greeted them. 'Hello.' She was more shy in her recognition of Van, but he smiled broadly. His public smile, Sheena termed it, somewhat sourly, but envied his aplomb.

'It's so nice to see you again, Cora.' He took her hand and held it for slightly longer than was necessary, casting curious eyes at the man with her.

'I'm sorry,' Cora apologized hastily. 'You haven't met Brian, have you? Darling, this is Sheena Hastings, you've heard me mention her often, and Van Goalan of course I don't have to introduce. My husband, Brian Gates.'

'Gates?' The name escaped before Sheena could control her surprise sufficiently to realize and she bit her lip hastily.

Cora nodded, her smile wide and enviably happy. 'I'm Mrs. Gates,' she said with unconcealable pride, 'since this morning.'

'Oh, how – how wonderful! I hope you'll both be very happy.' Sheena heard her own voice saying the conventional things and Van's paying more flowery homage to the occasion, but her mind spun madly round and round trying to imagine what Gwyn would feel when he knew. He was fond of Cora, she felt certain of it. That couldn't-care-less attitude he adopted did not deceive her for a moment, and she felt suddenly and inexplicably angry with Cora Gates, née Lindsey, for what she had done to him.

The day seemed less sunny, suddenly, and she felt less like laughing and talking so that Van found her unusually silent when they drove home along the coast road. What she would say to Gwyn, she had no idea, but somehow she must try and offer the equivalent of a shoulder to cry on. It was the least she could do after all the times he had consoled her, but the memory of how she had undermined his stand against letting Barbell be used for filming made her feel horribly guilty when she added it to the fact of Cora being married.

If Van found her less congenial company than usual he did not show it, or even remark on it. He was, Sheena thought ruefully, far too pleased with her efforts on his behalf with Uncle George and Uncle John. He kissed her

174

fervently to show her how grateful he was even though Mrs. Goodenough hovered curiously in the doorway, and drove off whistling cheerfully to himself.

Sheena was quiet at dinner that night too and her uncle looked at her curiously once or twice, though he said nothing until they had finished their meal. 'Is something wrong?' he asked as she stirred her coffee absently.

'Wrong?' she blinked hazily for a moment.

'If you're worrying about that Barbell business,' he told her with a smile, 'you need not. I've had a word with George and with a couple of the other interested parties and we've agreed that if we insist on proper restoration of the sands to exactly as they are now and a guarantee that the place will not be named in the publicity blurb, then there's no reason why your Van Goalan shouldn't make his precious film there. Subject to the agreement of the rest of the committee of course.' He looked across the table at her, obviously expecting some pleasurable reaction. 'There – does that suit you?'

'Yes. Yes, of course, Uncle John, that's fine, thank you.' It was even worse now, Sheena thought, for not only would Gwyn know she had been actively responsible for influencing both George Madoc and her own uncle against him, but it was now more or less a fact that she had won and he had, or would be, defeated at the next committee meeting. Poor Gwyn, he would be terribly downhearted with so much going against him.

She went down to the beach that evening, very uncertain what she would say or do, but determined to console him on the subject of Cora at least. She found him already there, but fully dressed and obviously with no intention of joining her in the water, and her heart sank dismally. Evidently he was taking it even harder than she feared, and was low in despair.

She felt guilty as well as compassionate as she walked

175

down the sandy incline towards him, but it was not sorrow that looked up at her from the blue eyes when she joined him, but anger – a glittering, cold anger like she had seen when those men had attempted to abduct her in Sandlea, and only then.

'Gwyn.' She sat down beside him on the sand, more uncertain than ever how to begin, her heart racing erratically as she sought for words.

'You *have* been a busy little Mata Hari, haven't you?' He turned and looked at her and she instinctively shrank from his anger.

'I – I don't know what you mean.'

'You don't know what I mean.' His voice caricatured her cruelly. 'Don't act so innocent, Sheena, it doesn't go with the image.'

'If you mean about Barbell—' she began, and he interrupted her impatiently.

'Of course I mean about Barbell,' he retorted. 'You went and saw Father yesterday and rolled your big dark eyes at him, to good effect of course, then you did the same on John, who's always given you your own way anyway. Well, congratulations. It takes a lot to move Father, I told you you were very good at the *femme fatale* bit, didn't I?' The extent of his anger could be judged by his use of Father instead of the more usual Pop, and Sheena felt as if she could have curled up and cried when he looked at her like that.

'I knew you'd be – be angry,' she said shakily. 'I – I didn't mean to behave like – like you say I did.'

'But you *did*,' he insisted. 'You deliberately set about persuading them to see your point of view, or more correctly Van's point of view, and you didn't much care how you did it.'

'That's not true!' Sheena denied indignantly. 'I – I didn't *mean* to act like that – it just happened.'

For a moment he said nothing, but looked at her steadily and disconcertingly, then he shook his head slowly. 'My God,' he said softly at last, 'I don't believe you do realize how potent you are.' He studied her for a moment longer, some of the anger gone from his eyes, then he laughed shortly. 'What are you going to do?' he asked. 'Work your way through the committee? You've already undermined about twenty-five per cent of them, directly or indirectly.'

'Gwyn, that's not fair!'

'Not fair?' He ran his fingers through his hair in a gesture of desperation. 'Do you think *you've* been fair? Van only has to tell you to turn the tide and you do it like a shot without any scruples about *how* you set about it or how you feel yourself, just obeying orders from the big man. All right.' He held up a hand when she would have become indignant, his shoulders drooped suddenly as if he no longer cared one way or the other. 'All right, Sheena, if that's how it is, fair enough. If at the next committee meeting they're on your side too, there's nothing I can do about it.'

'Oh, Gwyn, please, I—'

He shook off the placatory hand from his arm. 'Oh, don't be sorry for me,' he told her shortly, 'that would be the last straw. Go in and have your swim, only pardon me if I don't join you. I might be tempted to drown you.'

CHAPTER ELEVEN

SHEENA thought the following two weeks were some of the unhappiest she ever remembered. There was a lot she should have been pleased about, but somehow the fact that Gwyn so pointedly avoided her took most of the pleasure out of everything.

She still saw Van every morning and, although they swam less often, they still enjoyed driving or, whenever Sheena could persuade Van to summon the necessary energy, walking. They had been several times to Barbell Sands and Van had been full of his plans for the film he was to make there. His added excitement, she learned, was because he was now to be co-director as well as star, something he had always wanted to do.

It seemed almost certain now that most of the committee could be persuaded to take a more favourable view of the project and Van was so delighted that he talked of nothing else.

He was attentive and touchingly grateful to her for her part in changing the decision and he treated her even more charmingly than ever. When Sheena thought about it, she would have liked some more solid reassurance of his love for her but hated the thought of him considering her cloying and possessive, such tactics would never work with a man like Van, she was sure.

It was Sunday again and a fine, golden early autumn day with only the first hint of day time chill in the air. Van came for her rather later than usual, calling her out to him as he always did, with a short insistent blast on the car horn.

Her uncle eyed her speculatively as she went out and

Sheena frowned over his expression. He still treated the subject of Van with a cautious reserve as if he had not yet made up his mind about him and Sheena regretted it more than she ever admitted.

Van drove them along the sea road towards Barbell without previous consultation, Sheena always left the choice of venue to him, and she noticed the different colours now in the shrubs and trees, even this early on. It was the time of year for nostalgia, she felt, and this year she seemed particularly prone to it.

The sea was fairly calm, but there was enough wind to make sailing enjoyable and she found herself with a sudden and stronger than usual desire to be aboard the *Sea Bird* and skimming along over the water with Gwyn yelling the occasional instruction at her or smiling broadly when she did not move quickly enough to avoid a near ducking. Without quite knowing why she felt very much like crying, which was utterly ridiculous, of course.

'Are you daydreaming again?' Van asked as he parked the car and helped her out, and Sheena admitted it reluctantly.

'I suppose I was,' she admitted. 'It's a lovely day and this time of the year – I don't know, it always makes me feel a kind of nostalgia.'

'For the days of your youth?" he teased, and squeezed the arm he held.

'Something like that,' Sheena said, not prepared to reveal exactly what she had been dreaming about.

He planted a kiss on her forehead and laughed. 'Well, cheer up, my darling, because this is my last Sunday here and I intend to enjoy it.'

Sheena stared at him for a moment, her eyes wide and unbelieving. 'But – but I thought the summer season went on until the *end* of September. It's barely two weeks on yet'.

'It usually does,' he agreed, 'but the management at the Majestic agreed to a shorter run because I had other commitments.' He laughed shortly. 'I'm in a position these days, you see, darling, when managements are prepared to cut a couple of weeks off the run of their show for the privilege of booking me. It's rather a cosy feeling, actually.'

'I can imagine it would be,' Sheena agreed, and thanked heaven that her voice revealed nothing of the chaos that was going on in her mind.

There was nothing new about the scene around them except that suddenly it seemed to have an air of sadness that matched her own and was alarmingly affecting. It seemed like the end of a life somehow, something that would never be the same again. If she left with Van now, she would never again see Barbell in quite the same light as she did now and the fact that she had been influential in possibly changing the face of Barbell did nothing to cheer her.

'It's been a wonderful summer, Sheena.' She looked up at the good-looking face with its blue eyes which were very like Gwyn's and the summer tan which added to his attraction, and nodded. She had meant to smile, but somehow it did not seem so easy any more.

'It's been wonderful,' she agreed huskily.

'And it's all thanks to you,' Van assured her, turning her to face him. 'You're a lovely girl, Sheena.'

His kiss was long and passionate and left her breathless and she clung to him when it ended as if she feared he might move away from her. 'Van, oh, Van!'

His face pressed close to hers, his lips warm against her throat and her neck, he held her tightly and Sheena, looking with half-closed eyes round his shoulder at the grey-green sea and the endless sands, felt a tear roll warmly down her cheek.

'Darling?' He looked at her curiously.

'I'm sorry,' she murmured. 'I'm being silly.'

'Of course you are,' he told her gently. 'What is there to cry about? I love being with you, but I don't expect you to cry when I kiss you.'

'I'm sorry.'

'Don't be.' He drew her close again and brushed his lips against her brow. 'Just be happy, darling, that's all that matters.'

Sheena saw Van as often as she ever did during the next week, but he refused to talk about anything seriously, declaring that he refused to have his last few days at Lea Bay spoiled by anything more serious than having a good time.

Sheena saw nothing of Gwyn until the Saturday night when they were both invited to a last night party after the show. She suspected that Gwyn's invitation had been prompted more by good manners on Van's part than by the desire for his company, for the two men were obviously no better friends yet and were unlikely to be now.

The party was a noisy, confusing affair with so many people that Sheena did not know and Van so busy with being in such constant demand that she scarcely saw him. She went home with Uncle John and Suna as Van was busy with his press agent when they left, and he only briefly looked up with a half-serious apology for his preoccupation. It had not, Sheena decided on the way home, been a very successful evening as far as she was concerned, but no doubt Van would see her tomorrow and everything would be all right.

There was no sound of the summoning car horn on the Sunday morning, however, and it was her uncle who handed her a note after she heard a car drive off before she could identify it. 'What – what is it?' she asked, suddenly and horribly cold when she looked at the stark white envelope in her hand, and her uncle shook his head.

'Open it and see, sweetheart,' he suggested gently, some expression in his eyes that warned her what to expect.

Her fingers trembled as she slit the flap and drew out a single sheet of paper covered in a clear neat handwriting that, for a moment, swam hazily before her eyes before the words became distinct enough to read.

'Darling Sheena,' she read, 'I am probably a coward and you are free to call me one if you will, but I could not bear to tell you to your face what I'm writing here. I've had such wonderful times with you, the most marvellous summer season I've ever known and you've made me very happy, but it was not until last Sunday that I realized how much more deeply you felt about me than I intended you should. Perhaps I should have told you then, but lacked the courage. You're a very beautiful and desirable woman and any man would be proud to have your love, but, darling Sheena, what you feel for me isn't the real thing. Ask Gwyn — he'll tell you because he knows. I'm asking you to forgive me because I know you can. You've always cried on Gwyn's shoulder, I believe, but please, dear Sheena, don't cry too long over me. I will remember you always.' The signature was a large, flourishing 'Van'. Almost like an autograph, Sheena thought a little wildly.

She was uncertain what her reaction was at the moment, she was sure of only one thing and that was that she wanted to get away on her own somewhere and try to look at things sanely and without bitterness. It would not be easy, but one thing had already emerged and that was the surprise of finding relief among the many emotions that surged through her.

She put the note down, then turned and picked it up

again, without quite knowing why. 'I'm just going out for a while,' she told her uncle, and he came to stand beside her anxiously.

'Sheena, if—'

'I just want to be on my own for a while, Uncle John.' She smiled and was surprised to find it less difficult than she expected. 'I'll just drive out to – to Barbell, it's quiet there and I can think.'

John bent and kissed her gently beside her mouth. 'If that's what you want, sweetheart, but drive carefully.'

Sheena drove carefully, although her mind was on so many other things, and she parked the car almost automatically, walking down to the sands, lifting her face to the cool September wind that swept in from the sea.

At least now she would not have to leave Barbell, nor any of the familiar things she had come to regard as lost when she went with Van. She sat for some time on the lone vastness of the sands, sifting the grains through her fingers her mind seeking compensations and, to her surprise, finding far more than she would have thought possible.

She heard nothing of anyone approaching until someone sat down beside her on the sand and she turned and saw Gwyn. His brown face had neither pity nor scorn on it but only a gentle look of enquiry. 'Can anyone come?' he asked, and she smiled, almost automatically.

'Hello, Gwyn.'

She hugged her knees and gazed out at the grey-green water ruffled and frilled by the wind that lifted her long hair until Gwyn put out a hand and held it with a gentle touch on the back of her neck. 'You – you miss Cora,' she ventured, trying to sound normal, although she knew he would have been told about the letter, either by Van or by her uncle. Probably by Uncle John since he had come here to find her.

'I do,' he said, a trace of his old manner in the answer. 'I always miss my crews when they desert me.'

'I—' she began, but shook her head and looked down at her hand, the trickling sand slowly ebbing through her fingers. 'I was going to say how sorry I was that day, but you were so angry. I know – you were fond of her.'

'Am fond of her,' he corrected her. 'I've known Cora a long time and she deserves to be happy. I've also connived to keep her free from the nastiness of a divorce. Brian Gates was married when he and Cora fell in love and while his divorce was going through they dared not meet except on very rare occasions, so I acted the boy-friend so that no nosey-parker would get the wrong idea.' He smiled down at her teasingly. 'I never thought of *you* getting the wrong idea,' he teased her gently.

'I'm – I'm glad it's all turned out well for her,' Sheena said, and meant it. She had always liked Cora no matter how she tried not to.

'Bless you, Tuppence.' The endearment and the accompanying brief kiss on her cheek almost broke her self-control and she sought desperately for a safer subject than anyone's married bliss.

'You never did tell me what that peculiar Welsh name meant,' she told him. 'The one you said your grandmother used to use of your Aunt Blodwen.'

'Cadwen?' he asked, his smile wide and one brow cocked in query. 'I'm not sure I should tell you, it might bring on your fighting mood.'

Sheena shook her head. 'It won't,' she promised, quite serious. 'I promise.'

'Then you'll prove me wrong,' he told her. 'For it means "fair battle" and if you refuse to fight then it doesn't suit you after all.'

Sheena knew there was more behind the words than their superficial meaning and she swallowed hard on the

184

tears that threatened. 'I've no intention of fighting anyone,' she said huskily, and almost without thinking handed him the note that had until now been crumpled into her dress pocket.

He took it without a word and she did not look at him while he read it, but watched the restless sea and the soft ripple of the tide on the sand. Perhaps, she thought, she was not as surprised at what Van had written as she might have been, for there had been some niggling, persistent doubt in her mind for some time now, almost without her realizing it. Then there was that inescapable feeling of relief she had experienced when she first read the note.

She was aware of Gwyn watching her and of tiny pieces of paper flicking away on the wind. 'You didn't want to keep that did you?' he asked, very matter-of-fact, and Sheena watched the pieces flutter away, shaking her head.

'It would be all the same if I did now, wouldn't it?' she asked with a trace of her old manner, and he laughed softly.

'It's too maudlin,' he declared. 'And incidentally, the shoulder is *not* available for crying on, not over Van anyway.'

She looked at him in silence, at the familiar, comforting brown face with its blue eyes and the fine lines of laughter at their corners, at the wide, slightly crooked mouth and the stubborn chin, and knew that not least of her relief was not having to say goodbye to Gwyn.

'I – I think I knew all along that it was all a dream,' she told him quietly.

'Summer madness,' Gwyn agreed, and reached for her hand. 'I'm sorry, Tuppence.'

Sheena shook her head, tears starting despite her vow. 'You don't have to be,' she said, surprised to find herself drawn closer to him, near enough for his arm to encircle her waist.

'You're not going to cry, are you?' he asked with mock severity, and she shook her head.

'No. I've been a – a fool, and you must have felt like shaking me at times.'

'I could cheerfully have strangled you more than once,' he informed her blithely, 'but I'm glad I didn't.'

There was a strength and reassurance in the arm that held her and she laid her head on his shoulder instinctively. 'Gwyn, will you ever forgive me for – for making it possible for Van to use Barbell for his film?'

'I'll forgive you anything,' he told her softly. 'I thought you knew that by now. I love you.'

Sheena gazed at him wide-eyed, seeing again the face of the man who had come back for his lighter the night her uncle and Suna became engaged. The eyes a darker, glowing blue full of something that set her pulse racing wildly, the same excitement and almost panic she had run away from the night she had been lost on the sands. He had told her that night that one day she would realize what she had revealed in that drawing of him. What had been so plain to everyone but her.

'I – I didn't know,' was all she could find to say, and his laugh when he leaned over her trickled along her spine.

'Well, you know now,' he told her, and his mouth silenced her before she could find words.

'Gwyn—'

'Shush,' Gwyn ordered, 'you talk too much.'

Sheena looked up at him, her eyes shining softly as she drew a finger along the strong line of his stubborn chin and smiled. There had been none of that vague feeling of disappointment when Gwyn kissed her. 'I only wanted to say that I love you,' she protested mildly, 'I've only just realized it.'

'That's different,' Gwyn allowed, and kissed her again so that she did not even notice that the wind was cooler and the sun less warm as it always was at the end of the summer season.

FREE!

Harlequin
Romance
Catalogue

Here is a wonderful opportunity to read many of the Harlequin Romances you may have missed.

The HARLEQUIN ROMANCE CATALOGUE lists hundreds of titles which possibly are no longer available at your local bookseller. To receive your copy, just fill out the coupon below, mail it to us, and we'll rush your catalogue to you!

Following this page you'll find a sampling of a few of the Harlequin Romances listed in the catalogue. Should you wish to order any of these immediately, kindly check the titles desired and mail with coupon.

Have You Missed Any of These
Harlequin Romances?

All books are 60c. Please use the handy order coupon.

EE

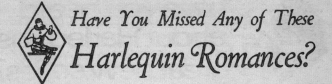

Have You Missed Any of These *Harlequin Romances?*

- ☐ 449 NURSE IN TRAINING
  Elizabeth Hoy
- ☐ 476 NURSE JESS
  Joyce Dingwell
- ☐ 906 NURSE MOLLY
  Marjorie Norrell
- ☐ 932 NURSE'S DILEMMA
  Hilda Pressley
- ☐ 941 MAYENGA FARM
  Kathryn Blair
- ☐ 948 ISLANDS OF SUMMER
  Anne Weale
- ☐ 950 KINGFISHER TIDE
  Jane Arbor
- ☐ 952 A COTTAGE IN SPAIN
  Rosalind Brett
- ☐ 954 DOCTOR WESTLAND
  Kathryn Blair
- ☐ 956 TAKE ME WITH YOU
  Mary Burchell
- ☐ 958 YOUNG BAR   Jane Fraser
- ☐ 960 MAN OF DESTINY
  Rose Burghley
- ☐ 962 NURSE MADELINE OF EDEN
  GROVE   Marjorie Norrell
- ☐ 964 PROJECT SWEETHEART
  Joyce Dingwell
- ☐ 969 NURSE AFLOAT   Jane Marnay
- ☐ 971 NURSE RIVERS' SECRET
  Anne Durham
- ☐ 987 SENIOR STAFF NURSE
  Hilda Pressley
- ☐ 994 JUBILEE HOSPITAL
  Jan Tempest
- ☐ 1001 NO PLACE FOR SURGEONS
  Elizabeth Gilzean
- ☐ 1004 THE PATH OF THE MOONFISH
  Betty Beaty
- ☐ 1006 THE COURAGEOUS HEART
  Jane Marnay
- ☐ 1010 DOCTOR OF RESEARCH
  Elizabeth Houghton
- ☐ 1015 SWEET ARE THE WAYS
  Essie Summers
- ☐ 1018 HOSPITAL IN THE TROPICS
  Gladys Fullbrook
- ☐ 1020 NO JUST CAUSE
  Susan Barrie

- ☐ 1023 THE SWEET SURRENDER
  Rose Burghley
- ☐ 1030 THE BLACK BENEDICTS
  Anita Charles
- ☐ 1034 NURSE MEG'S DECISION
  Hilary Neal
- ☐ 1042 PROMISE THE DOCTOR
  Marjorie Norrell
- ☐ 1048 HIGH MASTER OF CLERE
  Jane Arbor
- ☐ 1050 NURSE ADELE
  Hilda Nickson
- ☐ 1076 BELLS IN THE WIND
  Kate Starr
- ☐ 1087 A HOME FOR JOCELYN
  Eleanor Farnes
- ☐ 1108 SUMMER EVERY DAY
  Jane Arbor
- ☐ 1115 THE ROMANTIC HEART
  Norrey Ford
- ☐ 1131 THE BOLAMBO AFFAIR
  Rosalind Brett
- ☐ 1142 SECRET HEIRESS
  Eleanor Farnes
- ☐ 1152 A GARLAND OF MARIGOLDS
  Isobel Chace
- ☐ 1210 A FRIEND OF THE FAMILY
  Hilda Nickson
- ☐ 1230 CROWN OF CONTENT
  Janice Gray
- ☐ 1241 NURSE BARLOW'S JINX
  Marjorie Norrell
- ☐ 1277 STRANGER'S TRESPASS
  Jane Arbor
- ☐ 1292 FALCON'S KEEP
  Henrietta Reid
- ☐ 1309 THE HILLS OF MAKETU
  Gloria Bevan
- ☐ 1341 FIRE IS FOR SHARING
  Doris E. Smith
- ☐ 1354 WHEN LOVE'S BEGINNING
  Mary Burchell
- ☐ 1366 DESIGN FOR LOVING
  Margaret Baumann
- ☐ 1371 DANCING ON MY HEART
  Belinda Dell
- ☐ 1377 SISTER DARLING
  Marjorie Norrell

All books are 60c. Please use the handy order coupon.

FF

Three of the world's greatest romance authors.
Don't miss any of this new series!

ANNE HAMPSON

- ☐ #1 GATES OF STEEL
- ☐ #2 MASTER OF MOONROCK
- ☐ #7 DEAR STRANGER
- ☐ #10 WAVES OF FIRE
- ☐ #13 A KISS FROM SATAN
- ☐ #16 WINGS OF NIGHT

ANNE MATHER

- ☐ #3 SWEET REVENGE
- ☐ #4 THE PLEASURE & THE PAIN
- ☐ #8 THE SANCHEZ TRADITION
- ☐ #11 WHO RIDES THE TIGER
- ☐ #14 STORM IN A RAIN BARREL
- ☐ #17 LIVING WITH ADAM

VIOLET WINSPEAR

- ☐ #5 DEVIL IN A SILVER ROOM
- ☐ #6 THE HONEY IS BITTER
- ☐ #9 WIFE WITHOUT KISSES
- ☐ #12 DRAGON BAY
- ☐ #15 THE LITTLE NOBODY
- ☐ #18 THE KISSES AND THE WINE

To: **HARLEQUIN READER SERVICE**, Dept. N 308

M.P.O. Box 707, Niagara Falls, N.Y. 14302

Canadian address: Stratford, Ont., Canada

☐ Please send me the free Harlequin Romance Presents Catalogue.

☐ Please send me **the titles** checked.

I enclose $_____ (No C.O.D.'s). All books are 75c each. To help defray postage and handling cost, please add 25c.

Name _____

Address _____

City/Town _____

State/Prov. _____ Zip _____

N 308